Adapt and Transform
The Art of Self-Healing

by Jessie Li Hung Lee

Dedication

For my dad, the fountain of my healing pathways.

For my mother, brother, and sisters, Dr. Yu Hung and Dr. Mei Hung.

You are my role models.

For my children, Joyce, Austin, and Solomon, who encouraged me to tell my stories.

I admire the three of you.

For my ex-husband James, who has put me through my life challenges. Thank you for providing me with the experiences that helped me to adapt, transform and become an upgraded version of myself.

To myself, for surrendering to the power of the universe.

And to you, who are holding this book now and joining me on this healing journey.

Acknowledgment

Having an idea and turning it into a book is just as exciting and challenging as it sounds. The internal experience is from courage, while the external experience is from time and team management. With a previous dedication to my family, I especially want to thank the individuals who helped make this happen.

Thanks to Caroline Choi, who helped illustrate the book with my daughter Joyce, immediately without any doubt and provided support through research, proofreading, and graphic design.

Thanks to Patricia Greene, who possesses great tacit understanding and always provided friendly suggestions and immediate support from solid material to the invisible spirit world. I appreciate all the metaphysical and pragmatic conversations we have.

Thanks to Rita Andrus and the valuable times spent together in her studio viewing her green garden and drinking fragrant tea. In that quiet time, we laughed and cried through the book's stories and proofread together. You are such an excellent English writing teacher.

I want to thank *everyone*: all my patients, friends I have had the opportunity to heal, and those who allowed me to apply needles to them. All of your questions taught me how to explain things understandably; whoever said anything positive and negative to me, I heard it all, and it was a magical spell leading this book to exist on Earth.

Without the experiences and support from my healer friends and teachers, this book would not exist. Thank you to everyone who strives to grow and help others heal. Thank you to Dr. David Chang, Dr. David Chi, Prof. Fei-Hsiu Hsiao, Dr. Flynn Yi-Shou Chang, Gloria Xu L.AC., Grace Lee L.AC., Dr. Kun Liu, Dr. Lili Lin, Melody Yu-Ju Yang, Dr. Miles Minghua Wu, Dr. Ping Chao, Dr. Qin Fu Song, Dr. Yu Sandy Yan, Dr. Stephen Yen, Stephen Yu L.AC., Ying Wang L.AC. and great hypnosis teacher Yuying A. Lin.

To Laura, Jason, Justin, and Rebecca, thank you for being "chosen family members" in this life; you gave me a place to live, food to eat, and a safe place to gossip! I trust and love you. I will always be an "unkillable cockroach," as you said to me.

Thank you to my Mexican sisters and friends, Gaby Cedillo and Yasmin Cervante, who helped translate the book to Spanish.

Thank you to my niece Cindy Beyreiss who translated the book to German so that more people in the world can be aware of the self-healing journey.

Most of all, I want to thank the power of the Universe because I wouldn't have met any of you without this power or be able to do any of this.

~ On October 4, 2020, Red Resonant Moon, G.A.P. Day (Galactic Activation Portal Day), Blue Storm Year.

2 / 168

Disclaimer

This book is not intended as a substitute for the medical advice of physicians or other health professionals. The reader should regularly consult a physician in matters relating to his/her health and particularly with respect to any symptoms that may require diagnosis or medical attention. In addition, nothing in this book is intended to or creates a professional relationship with the author on any matter relating to the health of the reader.

Preface
Adapt & Transform

For me, acupuncture began as an act of desperation. I was in pain from spinal stenosis, a displaced vertebra and an arthritic back. This condition had progressed to the point where the steroid shots I had been taking were no longer effective.

My pain specialist doctor recommended acupuncture, and this is where Dr. Jessie Lee entered my life. Dr. Lee's treatment, through holistic therapeutic acupuncture techniques, was not only helpful, but the experience itself was educational as well. Dr. Lee is an excellent teacher. She carefully explained how acupuncture treats the person rather than the disease. The focus of acupuncture is the energy flow in the body. When people experience pain, whether acute or chronic, there is a blockage in a pathway of the body which affects the energy flow to the site of the pain. In the same way, acupuncture serves to redirect energy to a diseased area of the body and relieve the effects of a physical reaction in the body such as a stroke or heart attack.

Adapt & Transform is a fascinating book. It is filled with informative illustrations of acupressure techniques, acupuncture site locations and descriptive traditional Chinese Medicine theories and therapies. While the focus is on acupuncture and traditional Chinese medicine, the book does not discount Western medicine as Dr. Lee herself mentions her regular exams by Western medicine practitioners.

A most delightful aspect of Adapt & Transform is the biographical portrayal of Dr. Lee's journey and personal transformation while adapting to life across three continents and five countries in Asia, South America and North America. As we share this journey, we witness Dr. Lee's evolution as a healer. She takes us back to her childhood where she cured a newborn ailing puppy by channeling and resonating energy and carries us to her current practice where she combines acupuncture, hypnosis and psychology in a holistic approach to the treatment of disease and physical ailments.

Dr. Lee's life journey, as told through vignettes of her personal experiences, paints a broader picture on holistic therapeutic techniques. How she decided to combine various methodologies in her practice can be the subject of another book in and of itself. This determination was formed, in part, by her extrasensory perception attributes.

In the chapter titled "Walking Lightbulb," Dr. Lee describes how at age five, she witnessed varying hues of light auras emanating from people. Growing up in rural Taiwan, where her father was a Christian church pastor with acupuncture skills,

Dr. Lee was accustomed to seeing sick people visit her father for help. As the thesis research topic for her doctorate in traditional Chinese medicine, Dr. Lee chose "light acupuncture modality". Applying this modality in her practice, Dr. Lee occasionally experienced inadvertent flashes of the "walking light bulbs" (that is, people emitting a bright warm glow) and sick people emitting a faint gray light instead of the eye-catching light yellow glow.

The book is sprinkled with principles of traditional Chinese medicine. In several of her biographical sketches, we witness how Dr. Lee's fifteen year struggle with depression guided her transition from reliance on Western antidepressants to Chinese herbal medicine. From the perspective of traditional Chinese medicine, Dr. Lee was able to conclude that an unbalanced heart meridian and organ function were the main reasons that caused her depression and other mental disorders (because the heart controls our mind and spirit, and mainly the emotion of joy). And then, imbalance traveled through connected secondary meridians and unbalanced the organs, such as the spleen and stomach system. Integral to many treatments in traditional Chinese medicine is an overarching spiritual component. This is a component fully embraced by Dr. Lee and her spirituality is reflected throughout the book.

Some concepts of traditional Chinese medicine will leave the reader questioning the basic assumptions of Western medicine. Dr. Lee provides an example of a patient, a retired nurse, who was receiving acupuncture for swelling in her ankles related to a past automobile accident. The patient initially balked when Dr. Lee recommended a daily 20-minute soaking of her feet in warm water in addition to the acupuncture treatments. "But why? We only use ice," was the response of the patient. Dr. Lee noted that if ice had worked in the long-term for the patient before, she would not be undergoing acupuncture treatments now. Because it restricts blood flow, ice temporarily reduces swelling and numbs pain. Noting the teachings of Chinese medicine, Dr. Lee patiently explained that the body naturally maintains a warm temperature range and "warm water keeps our metabolism, digestion and all of our circulatory systems functioning".

For the Westerner, this is a book that opens an accessible bridge to acupuncture and other concepts of traditional Chinese medicine. Dr. Lee provides an example where she used auricular treatment, or the placement of vegetable seeds, in the ear to successfully help a patient manage her pain and quit smoking. By her own example, Dr. Lee demonstrated another dimension of traditional Chinese medicine. When she was in her mid-twenties, Dr. Lee became a vegetarian in response to allergies she experienced after eating seafood and meats. A little over twenty years later, she learned from further allergic reactions to her vegetarian diet, and lessons from her traditional Chinese medicine instructors, that she had to balance her nutrition by adding very small amounts of meat and seafood to her diet.

Balance, the Yin and Yang, and introspection, seeking the Divine, are the hallmarks of Dr. Lee's journey. The goal is to achieve "unity of man and the universe". Adapt & Transform tells the story of Dr. Lee's evolution to the person she is today. This book is a treasure for those seeking an easy introduction to acupuncture and traditional Chinese medicine. Readers will also receive a bonus as they explore Dr. Lee's life story and her continuing efforts to bring peace and healing to a population ailing from a life of imbalance. Thank you Dr. Lee for sharing your knowledge and your empowering story.

Adrian K. Panton, Attorney
Oct 25, 2020

Biography of Adrian K. Panton

Mr. Panton was born in Brooklyn, New York in 1945 and resided in the St. Albans area of Queens, New York through graduation from high school in 1963. He graduated in 1967 with a Bachelor of Arts degree in International Relations from American University, School of International Service, in Washington, D.C.

After a brief stint as a welfare caseworker, Mr. Panton, in 1972, graduated with a Juris Doctor degree from The Ohio State University College of Law (now Moritz College of Law), in Columbus, Ohio.

Following his graduation from law school, Mr. Panton moved to Los Angeles where he practiced law with the California State Public Defender and the California Attorney General.

His practice focus with the California State Public Defender was as a criminal trial and appellate defense attorney. He practiced administrative and civil law during his service with the Office of the California Attorney General, and retired from that office in 2007.

In his retirement, Mr. Panton has continued his work as a hospice volunteer for Southern California Kaiser Permanente and serves as a volunteer with the Pasadena Museum of History. He also works part-time as a court-appointed attorney representing indigent defendants in the appeals of their felony criminal convictions. Mr. Panton is a member of the First African Methodist Episcopal Church in Pasadena. He is active in the music department and formerly served as the Founding President of the Men's Chorus.

Preface
Love Can Heal

It is my great honor to write the preface for Dr. Jessie (Li Hung) Lee's book. In my heart, she is a Healing Master!

This book is a fantastic record of Jessie's life journey of how she transformed from suffering a needle phobia to becoming a skilled acupuncture doctor through many meaningful life stories she had experienced from childhood to her menopause. She is full of positive energy, passion, always happy to heal people, eager to explore, dives deep to understand the inner self, and is always thirsty to absorb knowledge and skills related to healing. Full of reflections about life events and connections to the whole universe's energy is all Jessie's natural spiritual self.

Western Medicine emphasizes persons' diseases, but Oriental medicine focuses on the person. The former is disease-oriented, and the latter is human-oriented. To explain it in-depth, Chinese medicine studies the three levels of Tian (Heaven), Di (Earth), Ren (Human), and how to harmonize among them. These three levels can be called the universe. The universe can be small or big, like an an to a human; it can be tiny or enormous, such as a small piece of sand or the entire earth; it can be micro or macro, a single cell or the whole galaxy. Jessie's book aims to tell readers about this sophisticated philosophy through her common personal life stories and how she's gone through thick and thin and finally achieved her wholeness, which is her own universe.

From traditional acupuncture treatment to color light acupuncture, from moxa to Gua Sha, from touch therapy to Tai Chi exercise, from aromatherapy to hypnosis, from diet suggestion to body constitution, from Wu Yun Liu Qi theory to quantum physics, and so on, her unique experience and special techniques shown in this book will blow your mind.

As people always catch some illness or suboptimal health status, varieties of treatment techniques are developed to help people get optimal health. Humans would be living healthier if we could harmonize with the universe, which includes people we interact with, the environment we live in, climates we perceive, etc. Through her life journey in this book, you would see the path on how she's often deeply touched with tears by realizing the valuable treasures that our ancestors passed on to us.

The road trip to achieve her current success was not easy, and she did get lost before reuniting with her soul. There are always ups and downs to life. The stories she describes in this book include both the good days and the dark days. Yin and Yang are two basic concepts in Chinese medicine. Besides happiness and success -Yang- in her life, the depressed and frustrated days -Yin- lingers as well. The tough days in her life made Jessie achieve a new level of awareness. She had gone through severe allergic and physical reactions, an early stage of esophageal cancer, years of depression plaguing both her and her mother, menopausal symptoms, and the loss of her only brother. Jessie overcame all her physical and psychological challenges through self-awareness, disciplined health management, acupuncture treatments, herbal formulas, emotional clearance, and many more. All these accumulations make her reborn and healthy again. She sets a prime example for people who wonder how to find a way to heal. This book also builds a bridge over to the Chinese Medicine palace for those who are curious to explore it.

I love the sayings written at the beginning of each chapter, which ignites my curiosity and drives me to read through. Additionally, I like the practical self-help tips at the end of many chapters, including acupressure, Gua Sha, herbal tea, etc. These are all very practical and can be easily applied. Moreover, her daughter Joyce and friend Caroline drew lots of wonderful paintings to illustrate this book vividly.

I was touched by the prologue, describing how she experienced her father's death peacefully and spiritually. I admire her calmness and how strong her mind is! She transformed herself from knowing little about acupuncture to becoming a great healer in multiple aspects: acupuncturist, herbalist, hypnosis therapist, and more. All these achievements were initiated by her father's loss and encouraged by the promise she made to her father. She has gone this far and will keep doing better. Her father in heaven would be surely proud of his three daughters, who are all practicing oriental medicine.

I met Jessie when we were both studying the doctorate programs of Chinese Medicine in San Jose in 2015, but I had known her elder sister Jennifer (Dr. Mei Hung) back in 2010 and was unaware that they were immediate family. It's a beautiful destiny between us in such a small world called "Yuan Fen" in Chinese. It's also a Yuan Fen to whoever has the opportunity to read this book. Please live in the moment and cherish the present, as the present is a gift. You have an excellent opportunity to know Jessie by reading her book, being her friend, or being lucky enough to be treated by her. You will know how sincere she is.

Currently the COVID-19 pandemic occurs while I'm writing this preface. According to the "Wu Yun Liu Qi" theory - a part of traditional Chinese medicine, many acupuncturists who knew this theory had already successfully predicted that there would be a severe lung plague starting at the end of 2019, which is named COVID-19 now. Jessie has been selflessly providing treatments to many of her clients to fight this disease. Health is prosperity. I wish her and the reader the very best in every aspect!

In the end, I would like to urge all like-minded people to love this world, love our earth, make our life better now and then, not only for us but also for our future generations! Love can heal everything!

Dr. Kun Liu LAc. DAOM
August 9, 2020

Biography of Dr. Kun Liu

Dr. Kun Liu grew up in a family of traditional Chinese medicine, and she is the third generation to practice Chinese medicine in her family.

She holds her bachelor's degree in acupuncture at Tianjin University of Traditional Chinese Medicine, China, and a doctorate degree in acupuncture and oriental medicine at Five Branches University, San Jose, USA. Moreover, she's very interested in psychology and came to the USA to study, and received her master's degree in psychology at California State University, Los Angeles.

Kun strongly believes that treating patients both physically and psychologically is the ultimate goal to heal. She is a licensed acupuncturist both in California and Texas and is currently practicing acupuncture and herbal medicine in Texas.

Adapt & Transform

The Art of Self Healing

2/168

We have to regain our self-healing power.
A patient in the clinic takes about 2 hours
for a session of healing. If once a week, it is
only 2/168 hours in the week. For 168 hours
we are with our body! We are responsible
for our health.

Written by
Dr. Jessie Lee

Illustrated by
Joyce Liu & Caroline Choi

Graphic Design by
Austin Liu

Contents

When I looked at a cup of tea, I said, "Hi cloud!"

Now when I hold onto acupuncture needles,
I say, "Hi, Dad!"

Dr. Jessie Lee

Prologue
Birth, Fading, Sickness, Death & Revival

On Mother's Day of 1997, I promised the Medicine Buddha, God, and the Omniscient Power of the universe. A promise that I would tell the world the stories of the greatness of acupuncture and about the art of natural self-healing. I vowed to bring awareness to the amazing flow of divine energy that resonates within us and teaches others how to activate this power for their healing. I would make Chinese medicine accessible and understandable for both current and future patients. But first, I want to tell you why I made this promise and how this book came to the Earth.

The day before, I received a phone call from my mother. She explained that my father was comatose and nearing death. Though I was in Taiwan, I immediately booked a flight to Central America, where my parents had been living with my three-year-old daughter. During the twenty-hour flight, I didn't rest for a single moment. I sat still, meditated, and prayed for my father.

At 5:00 AM, my plane landed in Guatemala. During the taxi ride home, it was so early that there were no cars in the streets. I looked up at the blue sky and saw the beautiful soft morning sunlight. It was lovely and peaceful.

I said to the power of the universe, "Please, please, please…You have always shown me the miracle of life, so this time, please show me your power again. Let my father pass fearlessly and with full serenity."

At 6:00 AM, I finally arrived home and headed straight into my father's room. He was there as usual on his bed, sleeping. I knelt by the bed, held my father's hand, and began whispering to him.

"Dad, I'm back! I know you can hear me. I know you were waiting for me since I was the last child to come back home. Don't tease me; I live on the other side of the earth even though your spirit may not feel the distance now.

"Dad, you will always be our hero, our sanctuary, and role model. And now, in your great moment of facing death, you're also about to begin the journey to heaven. I believe you will show us how to get there with bravery, peace, and joy. You've taught us to be kind human beings. You raised us to serve people. Now we're all grown up, and it's our turn to help others proactively without your guidance. You don't need to worry about us anymore, so get your trophy. I know you never liked it when people talked non-stop, so I'll end soon.

"Now I am here with you, I pray and only pray for you, my love will always be with you through space and time. Dad, I won't say goodbye...I will just say, until we meet again."

My father swallowed his last breath in front of my eyes and peacefully drifted into a deep sleep. There was a beautiful hymn around us in his room.

Time flew back six years, when one day during noon, I came back home from high school to find my father lying motionless on the living room floor. My mother was by his side, inserting acupuncture needles into his body.

"What's going on here? What happened?!" I exclaimed in shock.

"Your dad had a stroke and collapsed. He is paralyzed," my mother replied. "He asked me to bring his needles and put them in the points he indicated."

"How bad is it?" I asked. "Do we need to call an ambulance?"

I saw my father wave his left hand to deny my suggestion. That's when I realized he couldn't talk! I panicked but didn't know what to do, so I stood by and watched my mom put needles in him. After 45 minutes, it seemed my father's rigid right side regained some mobility. Eventually, he was able to stand himself up with a chair and head upstairs to his room.

Little Girl
I have a doggy and this doggy died, so I
don't know how to be not so sad?

Master
You look into the sky and you see a beautiful
cloud, the cloud has become the rain, and
when you drink your tea, you can see your
cloud in your tea.

Walk With Me" by Thich Nhat Hanh

During the following week, I watched my father put needles in himself daily. I couldn't help him do anything except stand at his bedside and encourage him to get better. And I prayed so hard to the Lord, to please give my father back his health.

My prayer was answered, he sent a miracle to our family. My father recovered very well from his first stroke by treating himself with acupuncture and returned to normal after a week. That was an incredibly fast recovery. He was seventy-two at the time.

Two years later, he had a second stroke. Again he recovered with daily acupuncture, but this time it took about two weeks. Another miracle had happened. But at age seventy-six, he had his third stroke. This time, acupuncture couldn't save him.

Three months before his third stroke, he was hit by a bus while crossing the street. It was a severe accident. He replaced his hip joints, and the surgery weakened him. A month back from the hospital, a cerebrovascular blockage in his left brain severely paralyzed his body's right side; he also lost his ability to speak. Since he couldn't tell us what to do this time, we didn't know where to put the needles to help him. We were scared!

My two older sisters and I realized that our heroic dad had become old and very sick. None of us knew acupuncture yet, and we couldn't apply TCM (traditional Chinese medicine) to help our dad. Father had asked me to study at medical school during my college years but I had refused, telling him, "No way, medical school is scary. I don't like seeing blood, cutting people, or even inserting needles. You can treat our problems, and that's enough." I was too young and didn't know how to think wisely and deeply. I didn't realize that my father was going to fade away someday.

Now my two sisters and I immediately found a way to return to school to learn acupuncture. Though we were in different countries, we had the same motivation: my oldest sister studied in Germany, my second sister in Mexico, and I in Taiwan. We were eager to bring our father back to his normal state again. Unfortunately, my father caught a severe case of pneumonia two years after his third stroke. His health only worsened from that point up until his death.

Will TCM and acupuncture solve all our problems? No, of course not. But TCM and acupuncture can be a key component to help care for and clean our bodies. They're also a vital green therapy that anyone can personally use every day for health care. We can't control the changing seasons, but we can be an excellent gardener to create our own beautiful garden.

It's never too late to take action, it's never too late to bring three new acupuncturists to the world. Our father must be very proud of his three daughters, who all became doctors of Chinese medicine. Now, it's time to tell my stories to my three children and you.

Childhood Journey

A Kid's Question

Acupuncture with meridian pathways are
like freeways in a city, or rivers flowing in
the land. It transports life-giving energy
that provides nourishment to every part of
the body; it also brings back our self recovery ability.

Dr. Jessie Lee

In the blink of an eye, time flew by. It has been twenty years since my father passed away. My children are now grown up, and my youngest son helps me in the reception area at my acupuncture clinic after school.

One day, a man with acute right-sided lumbar pain limped into the clinic. His pain level ranked eight out of ten, and he had difficulty lying down on the treatment table. I inserted two tiny needles on his eyebrow and decided to use a technique called "moving needles." I placed four needles in his left hand and asked him to walk around the treatment room slowly. Three minutes later, I asked if his pain had reduced.

"Yes!" Surprised, he nodded happily.

Twenty minutes later I took out the needles, he reported that the pain was down to a three out of ten. I set up an appointment with the patient to come back after three days.

My son was amazed and asked, "Mom, was there any medication on the needles? Was that why it was effective?"

"No," I replied, chuckling. "There was no medicine on the needles. Acupuncture works with the energy flow of the body called Qi. If there are blockages of Qi, caused by factors such as environmental changes, posture, stress, and imbalanced lifestyle, it can cause pain and problems to a person's health."

I continued, "The needles promote the movement of Qi, the energy in living beings' bodies. They help open the pathways that are blocked. Once the energy flow is engaged to its natural balanced state, the pain dissipates, and health returns. It is energy medicine."

My son has asked many questions about acupuncture since then.

The Meridians
Simplified Diagram

- Lung (Lu) - On Hand/Yin
- Large Intestine (Li) - On Hand/Yang
- Stomach (ST) - On Foot/Yang
- Spleen (SP) - On Foot/Ying
- Heart (HT) - On Hand/Yin
- Small Intestine (SI) - On Hand/Yang
- Urinary Bladder (BL) - On Foot/Yang
- Kidney (KI) - On Foot/Yin
- Pericardium (PE) - On Hand/Yin
- Triple Burner (TE) - On Hand/Yang
- Gall-Bladder (GB) On Foot/Yang
- Liver (LR) - On Foot/Yin

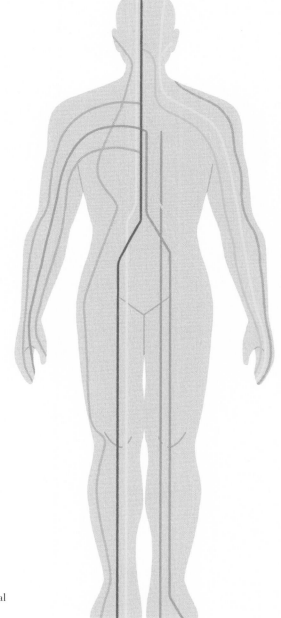

These organ terms are a functionally
defined entity and not equivalent to the anatomical
organ of the same name.

Needles

There is always a distance between what the eyes observe and the real experience. If you don't try and experience it for yourself, you will never know it.

Caleb Lee (My father)

My father was a six-foot-tall handsome man. Due to his being a quarter Russian, he didn't quite look Chinese. During WWII, he learned acupuncture when he was fifteen in Shan Dong's (山東) homeland, which lies north of Mainland China. He joined the military when he was nineteen and rose through the ranks until he became a lieutenant in charge of 2000 soldiers. He always told me stories about how he used needles to treat various illnesses and ease those in pain or panicking on the battlefield. But I never took an interest in acupuncture until much later.

The Chinese Civil War led to the Republic Of China, and the Kuomintang government lost the mainland to the Communists, leading to their arrival in Taiwan in 1949. My father was decommissioned from the army after he arrived in Taiwan. He had seen too much death, and the meaning of life inspired him to become a Christian pastor and serve in a small church that he built with his own hands nestled in the rolling hills of Hualien, on the east coast of Taiwan's lush green mountains.

He continued to use his acupuncture knowledge to help the brothers and sisters in the church. He was well-loved by the community, and tokens of appreciation came in steady streams. Fruits, cookies, and vegetables were always piled high on our kitchen table. I would stay by his side to observe and ask lots of questions. Despite my curiosity, I was scared of needles. Yet, there is always a distance between what the eyes observe and the real experience.

I was six years old and playing with some dogs in the garden of our house. It was a dusky orange evening in the countryside, with the night quietly approaching. All was peaceful until suddenly, my neck and head began to throb with pain. It felt like a sharp pinch and ached relentlessly.

I ran to my father and cried, "Dad, take me to the doctor! My head hurts so bad!" My dad was reading at the table. He took off his glasses and looked at me kindly. He replied, "No, you don't need to see the doctor. The clinic is closed right now, and our doctor doesn't work this late. Just let me put some needles in you."

"No!" I protested. "That's even scarier than my headache. Never!"

But my father ignored my complaints. He held onto me to keep me from slipping away. He took out some tiny stainless steel needles from a little silver box on the table next to him. He then sterilized the needle heads over a small flame until they were glowing red.

I was crying and yelling, "No! No! Don't put needles in me! It's scary. Let me go!" Suddenly, there was a small painless prick on my neck, like a mosquito had bitten me.

"That's it," my father said. "The needle is already in your neck. It's not that bad, right? Now don't move; just sit still. The needle has to be left in for fifteen to twenty minutes, depending on how bad your symptoms are. Sometimes we leave them in for longer."

I sat still and became quiet. I stopped making a fuss. My father inserted a total of four needles to treat my headache. Two were on the cervical point of "Wind Pool" - Feng Shi 風池*, and another two on both of my hands on the "Joint Valley" - Hegu 合谷* points.

Five minutes passed, and I felt my severe headache dissipating little by little. After around fifteen minutes, my father took out all the needles, and my headache was gone. It amazed me. I opened my eyes, curious as to how my father did it.

Why? How? I wondered to myself.

My severe headache was gone! Truly incredible! I ran outside to the garden to find my dog Cookie and tell her about this miracle.

Meanwhile, I looked up at the sky to see the stars glittering in the night. It seemed like they were silently trying to tell me something. That was the first time experiencing acupuncture in my life.

Father told me, "If you don't try it, you will never know it." It was at that moment I became a true acupuncture believer.

My favorite self-help tip for headaches

Use fingertip, a pen, or place a little
red bean on the following points.
Gently massage 3-5 minutes for each
point, a total of 10-15 minutes.

LI4 He Gu 合谷 - Joint Valley Point

Use this point for:
• Eye and nose discomfort.
• Head weakness.
• Common cold and flu.
• Headache.
• Stomach ache and constipation.
• Toothache.
• Fatigue, low energy.

(Do not use this point during pregnancy)

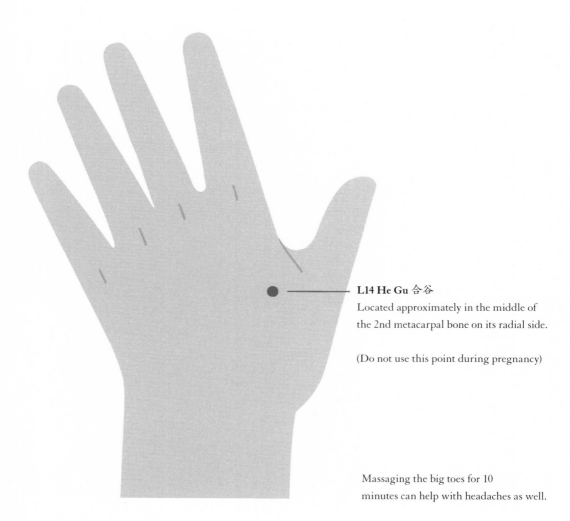

L14 He Gu 合谷
Located approximately in the middle of
the 2nd metacarpal bone on its radial side.

(Do not use this point during pregnancy)

Massaging the big toes for 10
minutes can help with headaches as well.

GB20 Feng Chi 風池 -Wind Pool Point

Use this point for:

• Headaches.

• Eye discomfort, blurriness, and optic neuritis.

• Migraines.

• Rhinitis and sinusitis symptoms.

• Common cold and flu.

• Sinus problems.

Located on the indent between the upper portion of the sternocleido-mastoid muscle and the trapezius.

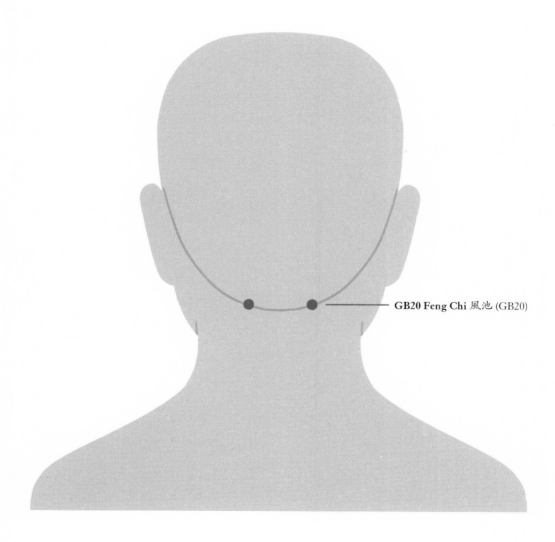

GB20 **Feng Chi** 風池 (GB20)

Touch For Healing

I treat what I need to heal. When I am healthy, the outside world is harmonious.

Dr. Jessie Lee

I love animals, and with my natural understanding of them, I would talk to the animals I encountered every day. My earliest memory highlighting my healing journey began when I was four years old, with the first stray puppy I adopted.

He was lost and hungry. So I fed the puppy rice milk and gave him my clothes to sleep on. The next day, my mother was busy with chores and forgot to close the front door. The curious puppy ran out and headed toward the street. Chasing after him, I called and desperately tried to catch him. But it was too late. He was hit by a car and died right there on the street in front of me.

I cried my eyes raw. After that incident, my parents felt terrible for what happened so they allowed me to keep all the strays I found. I happily took in all kinds of animals: cats, dogs, birds, rabbits, turtles, and voles. Despite being different species, they all lived harmoniously in our yard.

My father once found me huddled over talking to one of my pets in the yard. He smiled and said, "You talk to all these animals every day. Can they understand you?"

"Of course, they understand!" I answered innocently and sincerely, without a doubt in my heart. "I also understand what they say and what they want."

My father only smiled and walked away.

Out of the many puppies I'd adopted, there was one named Cookie. She gave birth to two litters a year, with five to ten puppies each litter. I was the only one allowed to approach her and help with her delivery. Whenever she dug restlessly at the ground, I knew that it was almost time for her to give birth.

To prepare, I'd make up a bed of warm clothes in a quiet corner of the house and keep a close eye on her. During delivery, I would sit in front of Cookie and encourage her to push. When the babies were born, she would lick the puppies clean of the placental membrane. I would help nudge the puppies close to their mother so they could find milk. And if she had a tough delivery, I would gently help pull the puppies out, wipe them with a clean cloth, and then return them to Cookie for milk.

When Cookie was twelve years old, almost a hundred puppies had passed through my hands coming into this world. No one had taught me how to do it. I just followed my intuition. Even though I was always reluctant to part with them, my mom left me in charge of giving the puppies away after they no longer needed Cookie's milk.

Taking care of so many puppies required a lot of food, and I wanted to help my parents, so I started collecting leftover food from my school lunches while I was in elementary school. At that time, I had 52 classmates, and everyone brought their lunch to school. At the end of the lunch hour, I would stand up with my empty lunch box to collect my classmates' leftovers, one by one. In the beginning, my classmates teased me and said, "Why are you doing this? You are like a beggar in the street!" It didn't bother me at all. I replied proudly to my classmates, "This is all for my puppies. The leftovers that are your trash will become my dogs' dinner. It's a win-win situation. I don't mind begging if I'm doing the right thing."

Once when I was six, I overheard my mother talking to the neighbors who came to ask for a puppy: "You have to ask my daughter – those puppies are her life, and you'll need to get her permission. We, as parents, have no say in it."

Although I was sad and didn't want to give them away, I knew we couldn't keep all the puppies. I interviewed everyone who asked for my puppies by asking their reasons and motivations for wanting a dog. My intuition was strong, and I was able to differentiate between good and bad potential owners. There was a custom of bringing a sack of rice or brown sugar in exchange for a dog. The rice and sugar meant that the family would treat the dog like their own family member. These were the people I'd choose to give the puppy.

Reluctantly, holding back tears, I'd hold out the puppy to the new owner with both hands. A few days later, I would walk or ride my bicycle to the new owner's house and stand outside to check how the puppy was doing. After confirming it was happy and well cared for, I would return home and let it go with all my worries lifted.

One day when I was eight years old, Cookie gave birth to a weak puppy. Despite his will to live, Cookie ignored and refused to feed him. Instinct told me that the puppy was dying, so I gently patted him and prayed over him nonstop.

"God, please save him from suffering…I know you have plans for everything, so if you want to take him back to heaven, please just take him quickly and don't let him suffer. If it's not time yet, please heal him."

All night, I was curled up on the ground, covering the puppy on my palms and talking to him. The next morning after everyone was awake, we found the dying puppy whining hungrily and crawling around looking for his mom. He was alive.

"You stayed up all night to be with him, and now he has come back to life!" Mother exclaimed in surprise. "Were you a dog in your past life?!"

I've always believed that it was God's miracle. Most people recognize this practice by the spelling Reiki, Quantum Touch, or channeling; there are different terminologies according to other cultures. It is a healing technique based on the sympathetic resonant vibrations in the universe and channeling a higher being's power through the direct intention to heal. Then we can understand that our body becomes a sacred energy field such as a holy church or temple.

Now, as a doctor of TCM/Oriental Medicine, a practitioner of acupuncture and an energy healing researcher, I like to think of myself more as a missionary to the body, mind, and soul. Although I don't follow any specific dogmatic teachings nowadays, I still always feel the love, gentle support and the miracle of life from above, which all give me boundless freedom. I believe in love and the power of the universe.

We teach what we need to learn.

Anonymous

Even at age five, I believed in the equity of all living creatures and caring for life. That's why I had to make sure the puppy's new family treated them well.

I laid on the ground with my dog Cookie at the end of the chapel. I told Cookie, "Don't worry, one day when we die, we'll meet in heaven again. Because you're attending church with me now." My father once told me that animals don't have souls and can't go to heaven as humans do. But I don't think that's fair. I insisted on believing in what I believe, but it got me thinking about life.

"All beings are equal." **First**, it refers to the heart of life, the fundamental as light, and we are one on this planet in the Universe, so we are equal. **Second** refers to one's thoughts and concepts; without comparison, no one is rich or poor; no one is smart or stupid; we are our existence only. **Third**, referring to thought as a being, all thoughts are equal as an energy flow, let it flow clearly, and reach the end of this life journey as one united with Heaven.

All beings are equal.

Buddha

My favorite self-help tip for healing with the hands

1.   Calm your mind. Using both hands, let Qi flow to palms.
2.   Keep relaxed and in a pure high vibration state.
3.   Focus hands over the painful region. Hold hands a distance of three-five centimeters for fifteen minutes. The painful area will begin to feel warm.
4.   Check results afterwards.

I studied more in detail from these books:

Quantum-Touch: The Power to Heal, by Richard Gordon

Esoteric Anatomy: The Body as Consciousness, by Bruce Burger

Walking Light bulb

Thanks to modern technology we have the
Internet, Wifi, and mobile phones.
Even though our eyes can't see and our
ears can't hear, we know those waves,
frequencies, and trace substances exists. It is
still a physical phenomenon.

Dr. Jessie Lee

Taiwan Yuli (玉里)

My hometown was a rural village with dirt roads not yet covered with tarmac. Bicycles and ox carts were common transportation. The town had a population of twenty thousand people and was surrounded by beautiful mountains, so it was always tranquil and flourishing with nature. The name of that town was Yuli 玉里, which means "uncarved jade." So pure and clean.

I remember vividly that our house was attached to a small chapel. There was only a tiny space for a living room and dining room together, a little kitchen and a small bathroom, and one bedroom with tatami mats where the whole family of six slept together in the bungalow house.

My father planted various fruit trees in the courtyard: peaches, mangoes, guava, grapes, passion fruit, and a lofty handsome pine tree about three stories high, which I spent most of my childhood time on top of. My father allowed us to climb the tree; in fact, he helped us by erecting a strong bamboo pole beside the pine tree so that we could slide down fast like monkeys. Later, I even made a secret hideout in the pine tree with books, pens, and paper, so that I could stay hidden in the pine needles for as long as I wanted. I would draw, write, read, and look down at the animals under the tree playing around, observing my pets playing and the passing pedestrians in front of our chapel. Sometimes, when I saw my classmates passing by, I threw small pine nuts at them until they noticed me. That was my way of greeting them.

My house was one of the three churches in the town. My father was a pioneering pastor who built that evangelical church with his own hands alongside a few construction workers. My mother was an elementary school teacher at the only school in our town. An atmosphere full of love, simplicity, music, and joy surrounded our family. I was the youngest in the family and cared for by everyone. My father always lifted me high towards the sky like a bird so that I would laugh out loud. I would always follow my brother and sisters to play outside and loved running through the grass to observe insects, lizards, dragonflies, frogs, and butterflies. My many small pets at home and the insects outside accompanied my entire happy childhood.

I vaguely remember an episode from when I was five years old. One day, I was squatting on the mud in front of the church, watching the ants line up and move their food. While observing, I grew very focused on the microscopic ant world. Suddenly, I heard footsteps walk towards me. Instinctively I looked up. I was amazed to see that the bodies of the people around me were immersed in white light. I watched some people walking by and noticed that some were surrounded by white light, some covered in a pale yellow light, just like walking light bulbs. It was fascinating!

I stared at this inexplicable sight with huge eyes, trying to ensure that my eyes were functioning normally. Being an innocent child at the time, I didn't think that anything strange was happening but felt that it was normal to have light surrounding our bodies! It looked similar to the saints painted in the church books' illustrations.

I often looked the books in our church. Even though I couldn't read the words at the age of five, I would observe the pictures. In these illustrations, I notice the messengers of God or Jesus all have halos around their heads. The light was always painted emanating from the peoples' heads, but the light I had seen surrounded peoples' entire body.

I thought to myself, okay, no big deal! If God and the angels have lights on their bodies, I guess people can have it too.

I took this ability for granted. After rationalizing the fantastic scenes I saw through my five-year-old eyes, I bowed my head and continued observing the little ants.

I also remembered that around that same young age, when I slept at night, I would hear the sound of water flowing. There was a small river about half a mile from my church home, but it made no sense. I sat up in the dark to look around. Was a stream of water running by my bedside? Why did I hear the sound of a stream so clearly even though it was far from my home? But being a child, I would completely forget about it when I woke up the next day and wouldn't mention it to anyone.

After I became a student at elementary school, I grew busy learning how to integrate into society. I gradually forgot those interesting sensory phenomena.

However, I kept seeing walking light bulbs of people during the following forty-five years of growth. They came as inadvertent flashes. I noticed that the people possessing this pale yellow light were kind and spiritual, a type of people who kept others close to their hearts. The light yellow glow is very eye-catching. I have also seen people emitting gray and faint light, and they were all facing severe diseases.

In 2015, when I was forty-seven and studying for my TCM doctorate in the US, inadvertently I had "light acupuncture modality" as my thesis research topic. As a response to my patients' request, they have often asked me, "Dr. Lee, is there any acupuncture treatment that uses no needles?"

I was speechless but kept their request in my mind, and that pushed me to do more research on the topic.

As I began to read massive amounts of articles and books on light spectrum, energy, quantum mechanics, and physics, I was amazed by what I discovered. The walking light bulb effect that I saw in my childhood exists in the documents! It was often called an aura in modern times, which has also been called protection energy or the "wei chi" in the Chinese medicine field. I found many images with the human aura, seven-color chakras, and other graphic materials. Auras change color based on health and emotions. Suddenly, I felt like I found a way to "go back home": the path towards understanding energy fields, spiritual life, and recognizing my identity.

Quantum physics discloses that the energy field effect builds everything up. I did Kirlian energy photographs to see my aura printed out. With today's technology's fast progress, many tools can now catch the colorful energy field; after recognizing this natural ability, I tried to train myself to read the different colors of people's auras to define their health states.

Another interesting vision experience that I had happened one day when it was raining hard outside, and I was in my calm, cozy studio. While concentrating on writing a report, I suddenly noticed that there was white fog filling up the extra room in my studio's empty space. For a second, I was wondering, what is that?

Then I understood immediately.

"Even if it is raining hard outside, it doesn't mean the inside of the house is arid. That strange white fog must be the TCM's term for "dampness...So even humans inside a building on a rainy day can still get affected by weather dampness that fills the space of a room."

It's the same situation that I believe many of you have experienced, in a dark room, we see nothing in the space in the room. But then, when a light beam shines through the window, we can clearly see that dust motes are flying everywhere in the air, even though it appeared empty before the light beam.

It's these kinds of experiences that have made me an open-minded person.

Diving Board
& Diarrhea

The internal organs consist of five organs and six viscera, which store our thoughts and emotions. A psychosomatic disorder may be caused and affected by psychological factors.

Yellow Emperor's Classic of Internal Medicine

During my childhood in Taiwan, there was nothing but nature. No technology, no cars, no asphalt roads. All were just beginning to develop. People wore clothes made of burlap, and children satisfied their sweet tooth with plain sugar balls.

What did I eat when I felt hungry outside of mealtime? I climbed trees and picked different fruits to eat. Often these fruits such as mango and guava were unripe and sprinkled with salt and sugar. Sometimes I'd even eat raw grape leaves, and those were the start of my stomach problems.

When I was seven years old, my belly started hurting often. I used to walk bent over due to severe stomach aches. As a doctor now, I figured out that was the start of my spleen and stomach system trouble.

One day I was walking around the house hunched over, and my father gave me a funny look and asked, "Why are you walking like that?"

"My stomach hurts," I said.

"Kid, you don't even know what and where the stomach is, and you're telling me your stomach hurts?" He laughed. "Don't worry and leave it be; maybe you just ate something bad."

He waved his hand at me and returned to his chores.

My father always had a way of turning big problems into small ones and small problems into no issues at all; he would try to comfort people instead. Now I think it was also his way of maintaining peace. I grew up watching my father treating pain and disease, so I did not doubt him when he said it wasn't a real problem. My stomachaches often came and went.

But an incident occurred when I was ten. I was one of the top swimmers on my school's swim team at the time. During one competition, I was on the diving board, ready to go. My teammates and family were cheering me on in the background. I took a deep breath and focused, waiting for the whistle to blow.

All was silent with anticipation, when suddenly I felt a sharp pain in my stomach and the feeling of a bowel movement. I panicked and jumped off the diving board immediately. Everyone stared, concerned. My mother pushed through the crowds and came to me.

"What's going on?" She asked, frowning.

"My stomach hurts, Mom. I think I'm getting diarrhea...!"

I managed to finish the sentence before dashing straight to the toilet; needless to say, I missed my race.

Ever since then, stomachaches came more frequently and was often accompanied by diarrhea. This condition is known today as irritable bowel syndrome (IBS). Any form of stress or tension would trigger a stomach ache and send me flying to the toilet. Especially during nerve-racking moments such as public speaking or test-taking, I would feel the need to run for the bathroom. I had to quit the position of class leader and choir conductor at school. My entire elementary school years were fraught with stomach aches and diarrhea until my family immigrated to Bolivia, South America, in 1980 when I was twelve years old.

Everything there was completely different. I had to learn Spanish from scratch. My father was lenient towards my academic achievements; as long as I attended school every day, that was what mattered. I thrived under the no-pressure, stress-free atmosphere, playing guitar and singing in a band, and reading piles of Chinese novels borrowed from friends.

During the holidays, my friends and I would drive a Jeep into the desert, the lake, or the streams. I even saw a UFO crossing the sky in the desert once. The stomachaches went away during those four years. In the natural beauty of South America, I grew tall, healthy, and strong. All these lifestyle changes caused a habit change in my subconscious mind, and that's how I finally overcame the IBS.

The cun is a measurement relative to one's body that is used to find acupuncture points.

One Cun   Three Cun

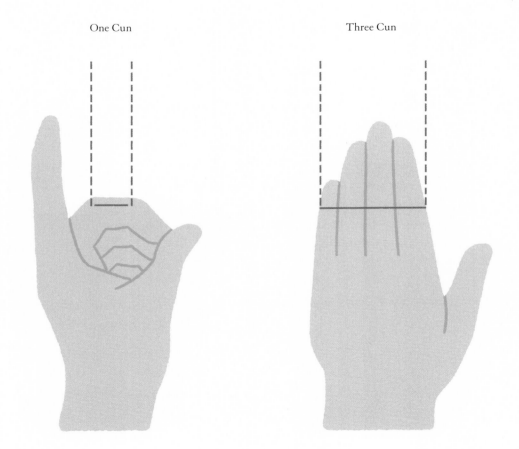

One Cun

One point five Cun

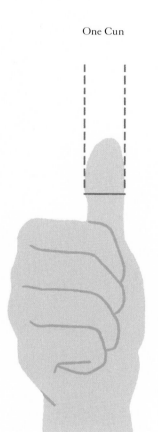

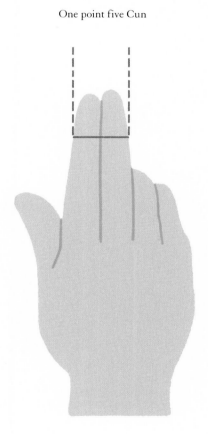

My favorite self-help tip for abdominal pain and IBS

1. Locate ST34 Liang Qiu 梁丘穴 (Beam Hill), ST36 Zu San Li 足三里穴, PC6 Nei Guan 內關穴.
2. Use a fingertip to press the area for 4 to 5 seconds. Continue for 5 minutes each time, 2 to 3 times a day.

It is also important that one learns how to manage stress and anxiety and reprogram the mind and subconscious to release stress. Dr. Bruce H. Lipton's speech and guided-meditation gave me a useful reference for reprogramming the mind.

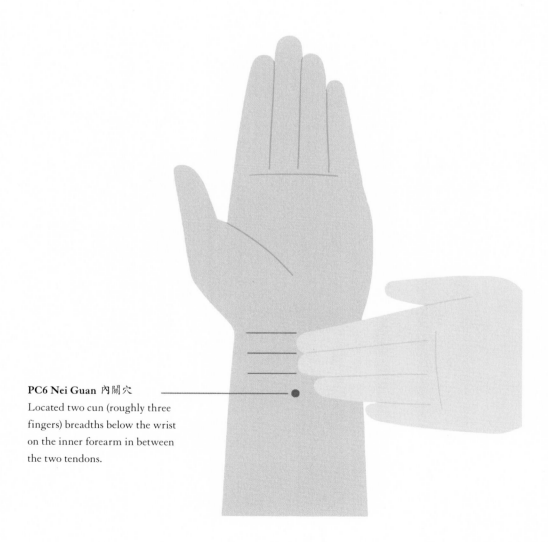

PC6 Nei Guan 內關穴
Located two cun (roughly three fingers) breadths below the wrist on the inner forearm in between the two tendons.

PC6 Nei Guan 內關穴

Use this point for:

- Nausea and motion sickness.
- Upset stomach.
- Headaches.
- Shortness of breath and respiratory issues.
- Carpal tunnel syndrome.

ST34 Liang Qiu 梁丘穴

Use this point for:

- Acute stomach pain.
- Vomiting.
- Chest/breast pain.
- Knee swelling, pain, and difficulty to move.

ST36 Zu San Li 足三里穴

Use this point for:

- Chronic illness.
- Stomach issues.
- Poor digestion.
- Psychological, emotional disorders like PMS, depression, anxiety, insomnia.
- Low immunity.
- Building and maintaining overall health.

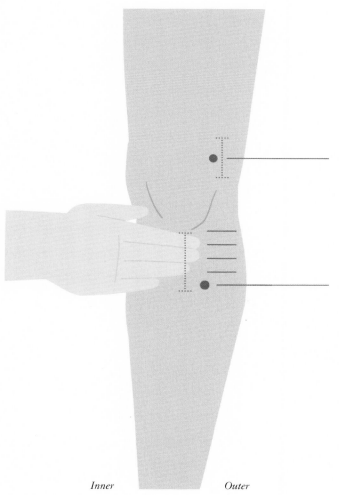

ST34 Liang Qiu 梁丘穴
Located two cun on the outside of the leg above the knee patella's border.

ST36 Zu San Li 足三里穴
Located on the outside of the leg under the knee, three cun (roughly four fingers) below the knee indentation, and one finger width lateral from the tibia's anterior border.

Inner   *Outer*

A Knee &
A Sack of Lemons

Gratitude isn't about giving and receiving valuable items, but about the heart's intention and the mind's thoughts.

Dr. Jessie Lee

Because of WWII, my father lost contact with his family due to Taiwan and China's political tension. My father was sixty years old at the time and hadn't heard any news from his family for over thirty-one years. He missed them terribly during their lengthy separation. The only way he could contact his family was to send mail from foreign countries. As a result, he moved our family to Bolivia in an attempt to re-establish contact with his family.

When we lived in Bolivia, my father served as an independent part-time pastor for the Chinese church and a full-time businessman to raise our family. We owned a small potato chip factory and had a few Bolivian employees.

It was lovely in South America. I still remember the scent of fresh grain, cows, horses, and the dust rising lazily from the dirt roads, filling the air with a natural scent I've always loved. The dust often turned the atmosphere pale yellow, blanketing the city. The sky looked so close it seemed as if one could almost touch it. It felt very different from Taiwan's hot and humid atmosphere, where the sky appeared high and impossible to reach.

One day, a nineteen-year-old worker from the factory approached my father. Tears were running down his face.

"Can I borrow some money from you?" The young man asked. "My right knee hurt so I went to the doctor, and they told me I needed surgery. If the surgery is unsuccessful, they'd have to cut off my leg! My family can't afford the surgery. I am scared and I don't know what to do."

My father replied, "Why don't you give acupuncture a try? I can help you for free."

The boy looked surprised and confused. "What is that?" He asked.

"In China, we used acupuncture to treat illnesses and diseases for thousands of years, including knee pain," my father explained. "With God's will, it's usually effective. Let's try acupuncture at least eight to ten times to help with your knee. In a month, if the needles don't help, then I can lend you money for your surgery."

The young man agreed. I watched my father put needles into not only his knee but also into his elbows, hands, and his back. He'd sometimes combine blood-letting and cupping too. I stood by his side and was always eager to help. My father would assign me simple tasks such as passing him cotton balls, alcohol, and needles. I felt proud that I was his little personal assistant.

My father treated the young man twice a week for five weeks. The young man's knee healed, and he no longer required surgery.

Later he brought his whole family - his father, mother, and sister to our home. They came bearing a sack of lemons as a gift to show their appreciation for my father's help.

I was surprised at the effectiveness of the needles. Even though I was only in junior high school at the time, the experience evoked my curiosity towards the tiny stainless steel needles. It left many questions swirling in my head but cemented into my memory the gratitude of the young man and his family - with delicious lemons.

My favorite self-help tip for knee pain

Locate the Ashi point on the knee, it will be painful to the touch. Use a fingertip, or apply a medical magnet or small bean with adhesive tape, or a pain relief patch to the area. Massagee the area for 4 to 5 seconds and continue for 5 minutes every time, two to three times a day.

Other helpful points include:

- GB 34 Yang Ling Quan 陽陵泉
- SP 9 Yin Ling Quan 陰陵泉
- EX-LE4 Nei Xi Yan 內膝眼
- EX-LE5 Wai Xi Yan 外膝眼
- EX-LE2 He Ding 鶴頂

Additionally, check the lower back and hip region for a painful point, then lie down on tennis balls to press gently to release the tightness. Use a heating pad on the painful area for twenty to thiry minutes to help promote circulation and reduce pain.

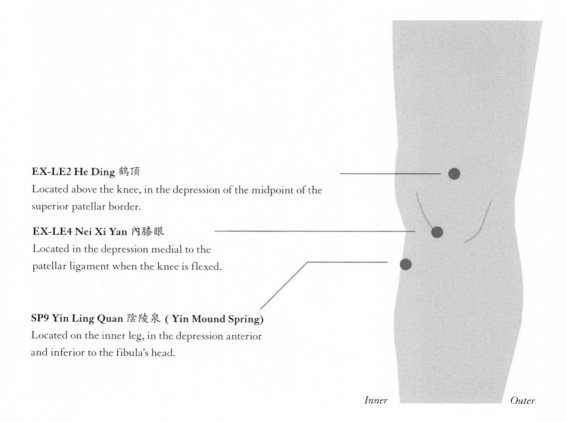

EX-LE2 He Ding 鶴頂
Located above the knee, in the depression of the midpoint of the superior patellar border.

EX-LE4 Nei Xi Yan 內膝眼
Located in the depression medial to the patellar ligament when the knee is flexed.

SP9 Yin Ling Quan 陰陵泉 (Yin Mound Spring)
Located on the inner leg, in the depression anterior and inferior to the fibula's head.

Inner   *Outer*

EX-LE4 Nei Xi Yan 內膝眼

Use this point for:
- All knee realted problems.
- Abdominal cramps, convulsion.
- Leg and foot pain
- Paralysis of lower extremities.
- Arthritis.

Special use for: sudden fright in children. Press this point until the child leans backwards, then stop.

EX-LE2 He Ding 鶴頂

Use this point for:
- Aching of the knee joint
- Weakness of the leg and foot.
- Arthrosis of the knee.

GB34 Yang Ling Quan 陽陵泉

Use this point for:
- Body sinew and soft tissue problems
- Cramping, paralysis.
- Knee, sciatica, and issues with the lower back, hip, and/or low limbs pain.
- Costal pain, gallstones, hepatitis, jaundice.
- Bitter taste in mouth, nausea, vomiting, and indigestion.

SP9 Yin Ling Quan 陰陵泉

Use this point for:
- Any water retention in the body, such as bloating, swelling, and urinary issues.
- Medial knee pain.

EX-LE5 Wai Xi Yan 外膝眼

Use this point for:
- All knee pains.
- Weakness of the lower extremities.

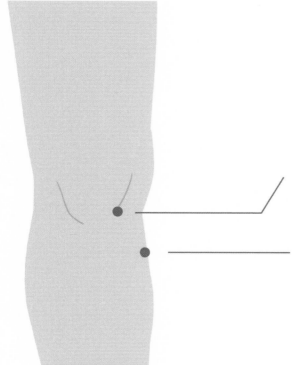

Outer   *Inner*

EX-LE5 Wai Xi Yan 外膝眼
Located with the knee flexed, in the depression, medial and lateral to the patellar ligament.

GB34 Yang Ling Quan 陽陵泉 (Yang Mound Spring)
Located on the outside of the leg, in a depression anterior and inferior to the fibula's head.

Exotic Healing Journey

Malaria

No matter if it is a white car or a black car,
or any brand of car, as long as it can win
the race, it is a good car.

Dr. Jessie Lee

We met the worst inflation in Bolivia that occurred between 1984 and 1986. I remember it was $1 = $b25 when we first moved to Bolivia, but in five years it depreciated to $1 = $b1,000,000. That meant in 1982, a bag of bread would cost us one $b50 bill. But in 1985, we would need thousands of $b50 bills to buy a bag of bread. Carrying sacks full of money, we felt like millionaires. But eventually, the inflation in Bolivia drove our family to Guatemala in 1985.

I was sixteen at the time, and I went to high school in Guatemala City. We had lost most of our money in Bolivia, so my mother went back to Taiwan to sort out our property there. My brother and sisters had already graduated from high school and college, so they were fully capable of helping my family's economic crisis. They would attend trade fairs in rural areas far from the city and deep in the mountains. Often they would drive a truck loaded to the brim with goods to sell. They would be gone for weeks at a time. Because of this, it was only me and my father at home.

One day when it was just us at home, I caught a high fever out of nowhere. My face and my lips turned bright red and burned for four to five hours. Then my body temperature dropped dramatically and became icy cold. My skin and limbs turned purple and felt frozen.

During the day, my fever would intermittently rise up to 39°C, followed by waves of chills, severe headaches, muscle soreness, and involuntary trembling. The symptoms would cycle back and forth between burning and freezing.

However, I continued attending school. My classmates watched my face turn bright red, then purple and pale. They were concerned and asked me if I was okay. I told them I didn't know, but it had been three days. The classmates kindly reported to the teacher, but the teacher didn't take any action. I tried to tell my father, but he thought I looked normal when I told him.

"It's nothing, don't worry. Don't be so nervous and anxious," father said. And with that, he sent me away.

"What? Nothing? Won't you give me any treatment? When my mom and sisters are back, I'm going to tell them you don't care about me," I whispered back. I was livid.

Then on the fourth day, my neighbor took her daughter and me to go shopping. She was a single mother working as a nurse in a hospital. When she saw that I had a fever, she immediately brought me into her house and took my temperature. It was 40°C. I mentioned that my temperature had been strange for the past four days.

"This is not good...Not good at all," she worried. "It may be malaria. It's a serious and dangerous disease. You need to go to the doctor."

"I told my dad already, and he said it was nothing and not to worry about it," I replied. "He won't take me to the doctor because he only uses Chinese medicine. Also, his Spanish isn't good enough for him to understand the doctors. And we have no spare money at home."

She frowned and kept muttering to herself, "This is not good...This is not good..."

The next day, my neighbor visited me at home and gave me a shot. She had mentioned my situation to her doctor, and the doctor asked her to administer treatment and observe my symptoms. After three days of injections, everything returned to normal, and I no longer had a fever and chills. I was very grateful as I didn't realize the seriousness of the situation.

Though my father would have performed treatments with his needles, he didn't notice my condition at the time because he was too focused on his business and finances.

Natural healing was a seed planted in my life at a very young age, but I do not exclude Western medicine's benefits. We must use different methods according to each case. There is value and a reason why everything exists, but it can be good or bad depending on the user. For example, a sharp knife can be used to kill, but it can also make delicious meals. Smartphones make everyday life more convenient, but they can become a serious addiction. Eastern medicine may be the right treatment for some illnesses, and Western medicine may be suitable for others.

As the saying goes, don't deprive yourself of food because there's a risk of choking.

Postpartum Depression

The unlearned can never compare with the learned. The short-lived can never compare with the long-lived. Why? Consider the small insects that only live one day. They can never know what a month is.

Cicadas or crickets can never know what a year is. Those are short-lived. There was an old turtle in the South of the Chu, who measured its life with the units of five hundred years.

In ancient times, a giant mahogany tree measured its experience with the branches of eight thousand years. Those are long-lived.

Wandering in Absolute Freedom, Inner Chapters, Zhuangzi (BC369—BC286)

I love kids as I love all animals, and ever since I was a little girl, I always dreamt about having five children so I could build my very own basketball team. So it came as a massive surprise that I fell into a severe depression each time after my three children were born. It started as postpartum depression (PPD) after each birth. But since I ignored my body's health, I didn't know that human beings have four main essential components that must function together: the physical body, emotional body, psychological body, and spiritual body. I didn't know it yet, as TCM theories concluded that our different organs stored different types of emotions.

The deficiency of the Heart, Spleen, Stomach meridians, and organs often triggers depressions, bipolar disorder, and other mental illnesses. As a result, I let my health gradually worsen as time went on. It caused severe morning sickness to me during my three pregnancies.

As a happy mother, I was so excited to meet my babies during all my pregnancies. Glowing with joy and happiness, I would talk and sing to the babies in my belly while knitting little quilts designed just for them. I'd tell them about the beautiful lives we would build. I was confident to welcome them into the world, or so I thought.

My first baby girl was born when I was twenty-five years old. Friends and family called to congratulate me, but I cried. Worry after worry plagued me:

"I don't know how to deal with my baby! She cries and cries; she won't let me sleep!"

"I'm afraid to bathe her. She's so tiny and soft like she has no bones, and I don't even know how to hold her."

"I think my baby has diarrhea! Her poop was soft and watery but yellow. What should I do?"

"I am breastfeeding her every two hours, but I don't know if she had enough to eat? Why is she always crying? Her diaper was clean. Is my milk not enough for her?"

After listening to my endless complaints, my cousin from Seattle grew concerned and said, "I think you have PPD. Maybe go to your doctor. The Jessie I know is always capable, happy, and optimistic, and this is not like you anymore."

"No! I never knew it would be this different raising a human baby," I shot back. "I'd rather have dogs and cats. At least animals let me sleep at night," I added grudgingly.

I got an infection forty days after the delivery of my first child. The pain from the wound aggravated my melancholy. However, I battled through it. The wound healed after two months, during which my strength and energy slowly recovered, and I was myself again. I quickly learned how to be a good mother and forgot about the PPD.

But the PPD symptoms worsened with each childbirth. After my second child, it took six months for everything to be back to normal. With my third child, it took over a year and a weekly psychiatrist consultation over that year.

Slowly the PPD turned into severe depression, and it smashed my seemingly friendly fifteen years of marriage. I struggled daily with body aches, fatigue, exhaustion, fear, and feelings of uselessness and hopelessness. I lost all hope and faith, and the world turned grayish black.

Overwhelmed, I was unable to move forward. But amid this dark fog, I felt an intense eagerness to understand why this was happening. During every moment, I was asking myself, "Who am I?" I desperately wanted to find myself again. I wanted to know how people could fall so deep into depression and become completely different people in such a short period. How can I be so happy this moment, and the next second I'm sobbing and unable to find my way out?

I remember the first session with my psychiatrist, Hsiao.

Looking me in the eyes, she said, "Congratulations! Depression is a valuable gift from Divine Intelligence. It's a treasure."

"I don't want this gift. It's not a gift at all," I cried. "I'm suffering so bad, and no one understands me. I don't even understand myself."

Still, I was a good and hard-working student. I completed every task and homework my psychiatrist assigned to me. She got to know my natural personality and my abilities very well. She pulled me out from the abyss. Later, she encouraged me to go back to school to study psychology, explore art therapy, and become a healer. Help myself, then help others when I could. And so I did.

After widening the span of life, I understood the arrangement of life.

My favorite self-help tip for four types of depression:

Heart and Spleen System Deficiency Type
Symptoms include lost appetite, low energy, fatigue, insomnia, crying, feeling hopelessness and/or worthlessness.

- PC6 Nei Guan 內關穴[1]
- HT7 Shen Men 神門穴
- LR3 Tai Chong 太沖穴
- ST36 Zu San Li 足三里穴
- DU20 Bai Hui 百會穴

Liver Qi Stagnation Type
Symptoms include a bad mood, easily stressed out, frustration, frequent pain in the costal surface region, lousy sleep, and wakeful sleep between 1:00 am to 3:00 am.

- LR3 Tai Chong 太沖穴
- LR14 Qi Men 期門穴
- GB34 Yang Ling Quan 陽陵泉穴
- ST36 Zu San Li 足三里穴

Phlegm Stagnation Type

Symptoms include a sensation of obstruction in the pharynx that cannot be coughed out or swallowed, sleep issues, restless sleep, many dreams, heavy body, fatigue.

- PC6 Nei Guan 內關穴
- HT7 Shen Men 神門穴
- ST36 Zu San Li 足三里穴
- ST40 Feng Long 豐隆穴
- RN13 Shang Wan 上脘穴
- DU20 Bai Hui 百會穴
- DU26 Ren Zhong 人中穴
- SP9 Yin Ling Quan 陰陵泉穴
- KD1 Yong Quan 湧泉穴

Inner Fire Stagnation Type

Symptoms include anxiety, impatience, a dry and bitter mouth, headache, dizziness.

- LI4 He Gu 合谷穴
- LI11 Qu Chi 曲池穴
- LR3 Tai Chong 太沖穴
- EX-HN5 Tai Yang 太陽穴
- GB20 Feng Chi 風池穴

See point locations in pages 74 - 76

LI 4 He Gu 合谷 - Joint Valley Point

Use this point for:

- Headache, head weakness.
- Eye, nose discomfort
- Stomachache and constipation.
- Toothache.
- Fatigue, low energy.
- Common cold and flu.

(Do not use this point during pregnancy)

LI 11 Qu Chi 曲池穴

Use this point for:

- Clearing inner heat, reduction of fever
- Damp heat skin issues such as redness, itch, hives, acne, herpes, zoster, etc.
- Shoulder, arm, and upper limb pain and inflammation; atrophy, tremors.
- Expels wind dampness from the channel.

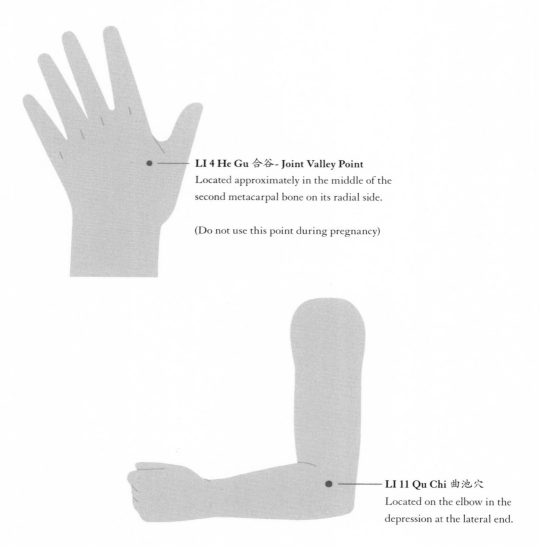

LI 4 He Gu 合谷 - Joint Valley Point
Located approximately in the middle of the second metacarpal bone on its radial side.

(Do not use this point during pregnancy)

LI 11 Qu Chi 曲池穴
Located on the elbow in the depression at the lateral end.

PC6 Nei Guan 內關穴

Use this point for:
- Relieve palpitations, chest tightness.
- Abdominsl pains, nauea.
- Carpal tunnel syndrome.

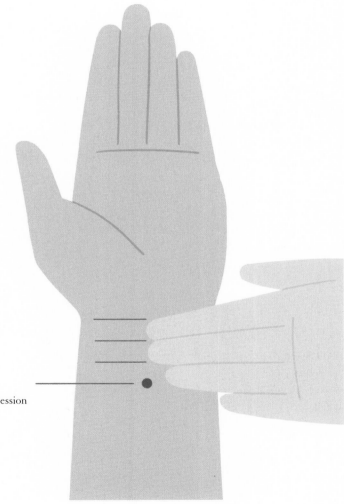

PC6 Nei Guan 內關穴
Located on the elbow in the depression
at the lateral end.

LR14 Qi Men 期門穴

Use this point for

- Depression, mastitis, chest pain, hiccup.
- Qi and blood stagnation, abdominal distention, hepatitis, gallstones.
- Emotional imbalances, anger, irritability.

RN13 Shang Wan 上脘穴

Use this point for

- Vomiting, nausea, abdominal pain, or distention.
- Emotional issues, insomnia, anxiety, palpitations.
- Gastric reflux.

DU26 Ren Zhong 人中穴

Use this point for

- Coma, apoplexy fainting, infantile convulsion.
- Acute lower back sprain and pain.
- Manic-depression.
- Epilepsy, seizures.
- Problems with olfactory. smell sensations.

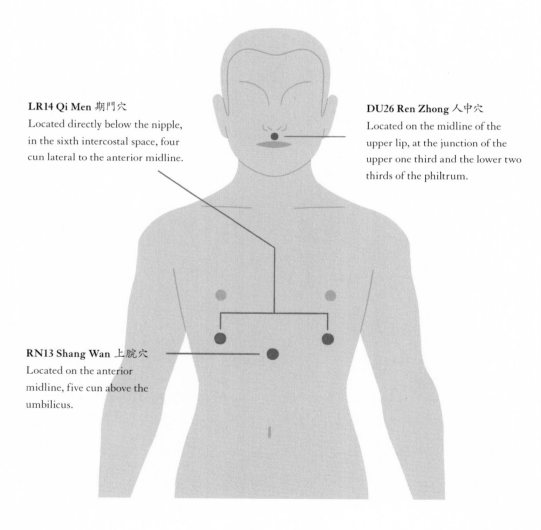

LR14 Qi Men 期門穴
Located directly below the nipple, in the sixth intercostal space, four cun lateral to the anterior midline.

DU26 Ren Zhong 人中穴
Located on the midline of the upper lip, at the junction of the upper one third and the lower two thirds of the philtrum.

RN13 Shang Wan 上脘穴
Located on the anterior midline, five cun above the umbilicus.

EX-HN5Tai Yang 太陽穴

Use this point for
- Headache, migraine.
- Eye issues: swelling, redness, and pain.
- Toothache, facial paralysis, trigeminal neuralgia.

HT7 Shen Men 神門穴

Use this point for
- Cardiac pain.
- Emotional & psychological imbalances.
- Insomnia, anxiety, mania, and fear.

GB 20 Feng Chi 風池穴

Use this point for
- Headaches, Migraines.
- Rhinitis, sinusitis.
- Eye discomfort, blurriness, and optic neuritis.
- Common cold and flu.

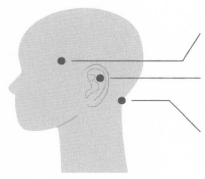

EX-HN5Tai Yang 太陽穴
Located in the indent about one cun posterior to the midpoint between the lateral end of the eyebrow and the outer canthus.

HT7 Shen Men 神門穴
Located at the wrist crease, in the indent on the tendon's radial side, between the ulna and the pisiform bones.

GB 20 Feng Chi 風池穴**-Wind Pool Point**
Located in the indent between the upper portion of the sterno-cleidomastoid muscle and the trapezius.

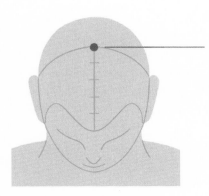

DU20 Bai Hui 百會穴
Located at the vertex, on the head's midline, five cun from the crown of the head.

DU20 Bai Hui 百會穴

Use this point for
- Headache, vertigo, tinnitus.
- Mental disorders.
- Low energy.
- Prolapse of the rectum.
- Prolapse of the uterus, vagina.
- Hemorrhoids.

SP9 Yin Ling Quan 陰陵泉

Use this point for:

- Dampness of the lower body.
- Medial knee pain.
- Any water issue in the body, like bloating, and swelling.
- Urinary issues.

ST40 Feng Long 豐隆穴

Use this point for:

- Headache,
- Vertigo, dizziness.
- Whole-body phlegm issues, excessive sputum.
- Cough, asthma, epilepsy
- Constipation.

ST36 Zu San Li 足三里穴

Use this point for:

- Chronic illness.
- Stomach issues.
- Poor digestion.
- Psychological, emotional disorders like PMS, depression, anxiety, and insomnia.
- Low immunity.
- Building and maintaining overall health.

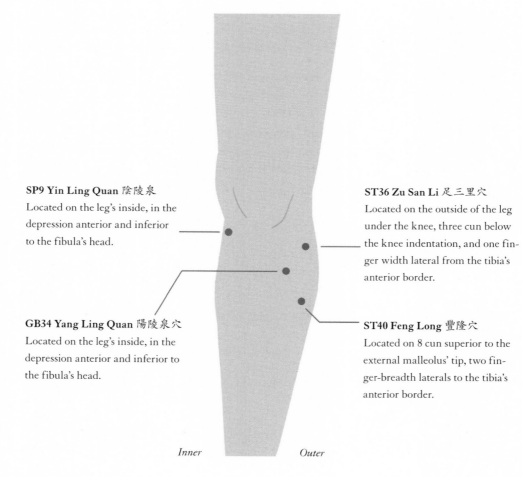

SP9 Yin Ling Quan 陰陵泉
Located on the leg's inside, in the depression anterior and inferior to the fibula's head.

ST36 Zu San Li 足三里穴
Located on the outside of the leg under the knee, three cun below the knee indentation, and one finger width lateral from the tibia's anterior border.

GB34 Yang Ling Quan 陽陵泉穴
Located on the leg's inside, in the depression anterior and inferior to the fibula's head.

ST40 Feng Long 豐隆穴
Located on 8 cun superior to the external malleolus' tip, two finger-breadth laterals to the tibia's anterior border.

Inner   *Outer*

GB34 Yang Ling Quan 陽陵泉穴

Use this point for:

- Body sinew/ soft tissue issues.
- Contracture cramping.
- Paralysis.
- Knee, sciatica, lower back, hip, and lower limbs pain.
- Costal pain, gallstones, hepatitis, and jaundice.
- Bitter taste in mouth, nausea, vomiting, indigestion.

LR3 Tai Chong 太沖穴

Use this point for:

- Depression,
- Headache, dizziness, vertigo.
- Insomnia.
- Eye issues.
- Dry and bitter mouth.
- Epilepsy, infantile convulsion.
- Uterine bleeding, hernia, urinary issues.

KD1 Yong Quan 湧泉穴

Use this point for:

- Mania-depression, mental, emotion disorders.
- Headache and dizziness.
- Blurry vision,
- Insomnia, anxiety.
- Poor memory.
- Dysuria, urinary issues.

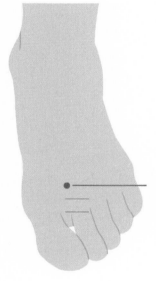

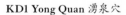

LR3 Tai Chong 太沖穴
Located on the foot dorsum, the depression distal to the 1st and 2nd metatarsal bone junction.

KD1 Yong Quan 湧泉穴
Located on the bottom of the foot, in depression plantar flexion, at the base of the 2nd and 3rd toes and the junction of the anterior one third of the foot.

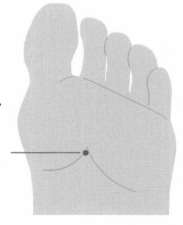

Ant &
The Milky Way

I cannot, but we can. We as the physical me, emotional me, psychological me, spiritual me, small me, enlightened me...every part of you and me.

Dr. Jessie Lee

My depression had evolved beyond what we might call the 'normal' state. My hearing and vision became incredibly sharp. During the spring, which is the rainy season in Taiwan, it would be pouring for weeks. Everything became wet and soggy, and the warm humid air smelled dank and unpleasant.

One night after dinner, I washed and put away all the dishes and settled my three children down. I asked my daughter Nena (a nickname in Spanish that means "little girl") to play with her brothers in the playing room, so I could rest upstairs for a moment before I had to bathe the boys and put all three kids to bed.

Exhausted, I locked myself in the room, closed the windows, and lay in bed in the dark. Embracing the silence and darkness, I imagined myself vanishing from this world. Suddenly, I heard a loud slam.

"What was that sound?" I wondered with slight anger.

Irritated, I got up and went downstairs to look for the children. They were where I left them, in the playing room playing their games.

"Did somebody just slam the door?" I asked impatiently. "Door slamming is coarse and impolite."

Nena looked at me like I was talking nonsense and said, "Austin went to take out the recyclables. He didn't slam the door hard."

I've always believed what my daughter tells me, so I wondered to myself, why did that sound so loud to me? I had lived in this house for fifteen years, and usually I could barely hear the door closing from upstairs. But now, it sounded as if someone had slammed the door by my ear. What was happening with my hearing?

I noticed that I turned my ear to hear tiny whispers, soft wind blowing, breathing, and quiet footsteps. Sometimes I also saw subtle bright spots floating in the air that wasn't dust. Soon I began to see the light around people again as I used to when I was six years old.

Whenever we had pets, I'd spoil them. They were allowed to sleep on my bed and were free to go anywhere they pleased. One night I snuck away to my room, trying to squeeze in a nap before my children summoned me again. Our cat Mimi was sleeping soundly in my bed. I tried driving her away so I could have the place to myself. Unwilling to leave the cozy bed, she ignored me. A surge of emotions came over me, and I started to cry.

"Everyone bullies me! Everyone ignores me! Even you don't listen to me!" I yelled at the cat before forcefully yanking the blanket from beneath her.

Mimi jumped off the bed and turned to stare at me. I still remember the puzzled look in her eyes as if she were saying, "Mom, what's wrong with you? I've always have been allowed to sleep on your bed."

Being a bit of a neat freak, I couldn't stand the house being out of order. I was forever cleaning. Even the dusty leaves of our house plants had to be cleaned one by one. I also spoiled my kids like I spoiled my pets. I tried my best to do all that they asked of me, but in my exhausted state, I couldn't stand them calling, "Mom! Mom! Mom!" Day in and day out, especially with my six-month-old son. I was frequently worn out and wanted to throw the noisy children out the window. These confusing thoughts scared me.

Luckily I was able to keep my rationality and sensibility by reading. I read books to understand depression, asked for medical help, and went to therapy. I also read lots of books about the unconscious world and psychology, and I often thought of space.

One day while cleaning the house, I saw a tiny ant run across the table. I bent down and observed it closely. Then I started talking to it.

"Hi, little ant, why are you so busy?" I asked. "You can't see me even when I'm by your side because I'm too big and beyond your sight and knowledge. You probably don't even know I'm watching you."

Amused, I chuckled to myself and continued talking to the ant. "You don't know that you're on a table and that the table is in a living room. Outside of the living room, there's a street, a city, and planes that can fly to other countries."

And then I suddenly had an insight. I thought, "Maybe I'm like this ant, perhaps right this moment, giants are watching and talking to me, but I can't see or hear them."

I felt great relief thinking of a universe that's much bigger than me, and out of my control, just like the little ant.

One of my family members is a psychic who can channel the spirit world to help resolve life problems. Spirits provide him with this knowledge by communicating with him through written golden scriptures that appear in his mind. This psychic is like a brother to me, and he took notice of my depressed state.

"Sister, I feel you have troubles in your life recently. Would you like me to help? I can ask the higher beings to help resolve your problem," this brother offered to me one night while we were at his apartment for a family gathering.

"Thank you, but I don't need your help. I'm okay now," I replied.

Honestly, I was skeptical of what he claimed he could do. But my other family members encouraged and pushed me to try. I reluctantly agreed and said, "Fine, but don't take too long. I have to feed my baby son in twenty minutes."

We stepped into the family room and sat down, facing each other on the meditation cushion. He instructed me to close my eyes and take a few deep breaths. A minute passed, and all was quiet.

Then he said, "The spirit of a Saint is with us now. He tells me that you are a good person and that everything will be fine in a few months. But with his help, you can go through this 'midterm exam' life lesson much faster."

I was intrigued but still skeptical, so I responded arrogantly, "Thank you for offering your help. But as you say, this is my life lesson, so I am willing to take time and face it. I will learn hard and fast. I just need some wisdom."

The conversation with the spirit continued. I asked questions about how to trust, forgive, and more. In turn, the energy would answer with images of nature, mountains, trees, flowers, and wind, trying to explain the truth of life to me.

About twenty minutes in, I wanted to end the conversation. But my brother said, "It's not that I don't want to stop. But the Saint is still showing golden scriptures that need conveying to you. He's not finished yet."

So the conversation went on, but I felt anxious, my baby could be waiting for me.

Suddenly, everything stopped. No more images, no more golden scriptures. Only a deep silence between us. The next moment, my brother saw a picture of the Milky Way.

Brother said, "Milky Way? I don't know what that means; there is no scripture explaining it." He described the image he saw, and from his description, I saw the Milky Way vividly in my mind. I kept silent. It was a spectacular view I saw in my mind.

Then he said, "I see a little ant in the corner watching the Milky Way, and it's becoming bigger and bigger." I saw it too; it was just like watching a movie!

With that, I laughed out loud until tears filled my eyes. I said happily, "I understand now, I know what that means! We have done it, we can leave the conversation now."

He opened his eyes and responded, "The Saint has gone. We are finished." He paused for a moment before asking, "You know what that last image means? Because I am confused, and I can't explain it to you."

"Yes! Let me explain," I said. "The last image is 'Divinity,' trying to reinforce me and encourage me to believe in higher beings. Because during the entire conversation, the saint knew some part of me was skeptical and didn't trust what you were telling me. All I knew was that no one knows if they're good or bad, so it might be best for me to keep some distance."

I continued explaining: "I grew up in a Christian family and went to church every weekend, and I thought I had a strong belief. But I didn't realize that until now – I doubted that there was a higher power. It's like theory and practice. Knowing about a thing doesn't mean you have experienced it." It means - be honest and then back up your words with actions.

I told my relative that his last image shocked me because I hadn't told anyone about the conversation I had with the little ant only a week ago. The Saint showed me that image to prove that he was a real higher being and always here with me. He knew my thoughts and problems in certain layers because we're all connected, and all I had to do was learn my life lesson modestly.

I concluded my reflections. "Everything in existence has its value, even a tiny ant. It's like standing on a higher vantage point in the galaxy looking down at present problems; the problems become nothing. Once I learn the difference between internal and external, and once I learn what honor and humiliation are, I'll know clearly who and where I truly am."

The knot in my heart untied, and I found my way back to my inner self. When we walked back into the living room, ninety minutes had passed, when I thought it had been only twenty-five minutes.

My favorite self-help tip for depression and sleep

Using the auricular technique, locate and apply some vegetable seeds on these ear points, massage gently throughout the day:

- Spleen 脾
- Shen Meng 神門
- Heart 心
- Anxious 身心穴
- Liver 肝
- Nervous Subcortex 神經皮質
- Occiput 枕

Also, I took herbal tea to help with depression. (Consult your TCM doctors for detailed information.)

How to prepare TCM herbal tea:
Boil raw herbs with water over the herbs and cook for 30-40 minutes; take two times a day. Always separate one hour with other medications or vitamins, do not take them together.

I am grateful to be able to combine acupuncture, herbs, and psychiatrists to help me recover from my depression.

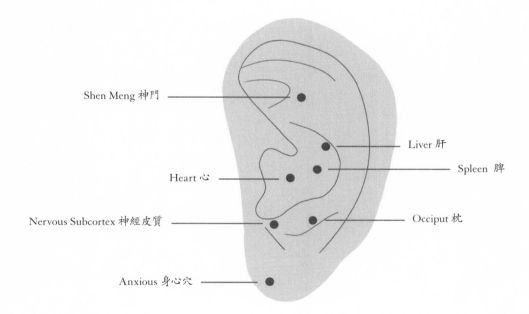

Lying
On A Cloud

I looked into natural therapies, energy
medicine and acupuncture. But I found
healing deep inside, within my own power.

Once someone discovers who they are, a
being of the universe, they are awakened
and gain knowledge to their existence.

Then they are able to heal and nourish
themselves physically, mentally and
psychologically.

Dr. Jessie Lee

In 2003, due to my severe depression, I received psychiatric medication and psychotherapy once a week for a year. My mood swings slowly stabilized. I became curious about mental health and the inner world and how these affect our physical health.

Under the strong encouragement of my psychiatrist Hsiao, I went back to school to study psychology while recovering from depression. It was a two-year nighttime course at a university in Taiwan. During the day, I worked as a program director and an art teacher at a bilingual international school, and at night I studied.

I was pleased with the psychology program and quite eager to learn. Although the psychology courses' information helped me rebuild my world effectively, I was physically exhausting myself between work, family, and school. But I was stubborn, I can do it! So I completed the semester.

Our last class was on the topic of career planning and consultation. The professor walked into the classroom and announced, "Today, we are going to do something different. Leave the textbooks and all the theories behind. We are going to experiment, something that might be useful in your future careers." All twenty-three students in the class sat up attentively.

"I believe you all have heard about hypnosis," the professor continued. "Tonight, I am going to use a technique called Guided Meditation. Just follow my instructions and stay seated." Everyone stirred with excitement. We were looking forward to a relaxing class without learning textbook-heavy, rigid theories. Our professor asked us to stand up for five minutes for a relaxation exercise, to move our heads from side to side gently, to shake our feet, to rotate our arms.

"Alright, you may take a seat. Close your eyes, take a deep breath," the professor announced. "Now, I want you to imagine yourself on a cloud in the sky. What are you doing up in the sky? What is your posture like?"

With my eyes closed, I rolled my eyes in my head and thought, what a stupid experiment, how could I possibly be on a cloud? I would have fallen to my death immediately.

But just as I was thinking that, I suddenly saw myself lying down with my arms and feet wide open on a soft puffy cloud, floating in the sky like a happy little girl. The imagery caught me off guard, so I adjusted my posture, straightened my back, and began to take the professor's instructions seriously.

"Now, it's been a week in the clouds, it is morning. You have just woken up from a restful sleep. What's the first thing you see when you open your eyes?" The professor asked.

"Now you get out of bed, go to brush your teeth, and have breakfast. What is the food you are eating?

"After breakfast, you go to work or go out for some errands. What kind of transportation do you take? Do you walk? Drive? Take the bus or a taxi?"

"Time fast forwards to one month later...

"Time fast forwards to one year later...

"Time fast forwards five years later...

"Time fast forwards ten years later...

"Time fast forwards to the end of your life. How old will you be? What are you doing? Are you satisfied with your journey?"

It was a transcendental experience, like watching a movie. I followed the professor's instructions and saw my life flash by until I was eighty-five years old. In one year, I saw myself in a Western country where there were many tall trees, and I had a school teaching job. In five years, I saw myself driving a white car into a school campus, and everyone greeting me like I was their superior. Ten years, I saw myself dressed in a Master's or Doctor's graduation gown and standing on a stage giving a speech. At eighty-five years old, I saw myself sitting in front of a table, writing stories, surrounded by cats and dogs, and a comforting sense that my children are close by.

That night I cried tears of joy all the way back home after class. What I saw was like a movie. All this time, I thought I had no future. But now I knew that wasn't true. I knew I could find the best of myself as long as I wasn't scared. Take action; take one step out of the comfort zone. I knew that my future was waiting for me.

After the night my life journey flashed before me, I did take action to create my future. Looking back now, I mostly met with what I saw in my inner vision in the class: in 2005, I worked as an academic director in Mexico City with many tall trees; in 2008, I became a school principal and drove a white car and students greeted me; in 2014, I got a master's degree in TCM and gave a speech in the graduation ceremony. In 2017, I wore a doctorate gown in the beautiful Silicon Valley.

Acupuncture Practitioner Journey

Again,
Headache

There is nothing to fear
but fear itself.

Franklin D. Roosevelt

To see other people doing well at something does not mean one can do it the same way. To talk about something is always easier than doing it. When I watched my father insert needles into people and heal them, I had a proud feeling in my heart, but I found it very frightening when I am the one to hold a tiny needle in my hand.

After my father passed away, my go-to for acupuncture treatments were my two older sisters. They are both acupuncture practitioners in Germany and Mexico. I hesitated to return to school for acupuncture because I had a needle phobia. I couldn't touch needles or hold them. They scared me to death. But my sisters urged me on because they were concerned about my health.

"You have to learn acupuncture and Chinese medicine as soon as possible! Your health condition is so bad, and you need to learn to heal and take care of yourself better," my sisters exclaimed.

Finally, I followed in my sister's footsteps and enrolled myself in classes with the enlightening mentor Dr. Song QinFu, a vice-president of General TCM Hospital of Yantai, China. Dr. Song went to teach TCM in Mexican universities for more than twenty years. I remembered even after a year of studying acupuncture, I still refused to touch needles.

One day, it was time for a change. There was a ten-day winter break, and none of my sisters were home. They were on vacation with their families. A severe headache hit me from out of nowhere, just like the one I had when I was six years old.

I took an NSAID painkiller, which not only didn't work at the time but gave me an upset stomach on top of the headache. I took deep breaths, performed acupressure on my head, and wrapped my head in a warm mat. I tried all the natural ways to relieve the pain but to no avail. Anxiety grew because I didn't want to waste my vacation feeling sick. I called my sister in desperation.

My sister advised, "Just put needles in yourself, on the Feng Chi neck point. The headache will go away immediately." Interestingly, these are the same points my father had used to cure my headache when I was six.

That which does not kill us
makes us stronger.

Nietzsche

"But I'm scared of needles," I told her. "How can I put them in by myself?!" My sister gave me instructions and encouraged me to try anyway.

I thought to myself, Well, okay, look at it like this. Right now, I have no one to help me to treat me. I'll just have to try it to help myself.

To relax, I took a warm bath, turned on my favorite lamp in the living room, put on my favorite music, lit some candles, and made myself comfortable on the sofa. I took out my one-time use acupuncture needles and located the sore point on my neck (in the intersection of the sternocleidomastoid muscle and the occipital). Okay, found it, I thought to myself. Take a deep breath. One, two, three.

I inserted the needle in my neck by myself, and it didn't hurt! The pain wasn't as bad as I had anticipated it to be. Acupuncture needles don't hurt in the way hypodermic needles do. I slowly inserted the needle to the depth it is required to take effect and let it sit for twenty minutes.

I felt at peace. I looked out the window and saw the lush green trees swaying slightly in the breeze. Everything became silent at that moment. The pain began to fade within five minutes of inserting the needle. I felt so proud that I had finally conquered my irrational fear and treated myself.

My headache had turned the light onto my self-healing; the crisis was a blessing in disguise, forcing me to step out of my comfort zone. I was one step closer to becoming a practitioner of acupuncture.

My favorite self-help tip for headaches

Guasha

1. Scrape in the direction illustrated below from the GB20 Feng Chi point down to the shoulder and scapular region. Use baby oil, herbal oil, or gua sha oil for the best results.
2. Scrape 5 to 10 times and stop, or stop when red marks begin to show.
3. Put a heating pad on the scraped area for fifteen to twenty minutes.
4. Apply one drop of therapeutic peppermint essential oil onto the scraped area.

GB 20 Feng Chi 風池穴

Use this point for

- Headaches, Migraines.
- Rhinitis, sinusitis.
- Eye discomfort, blurriness, and optic neuritis.
- Common cold and flu.

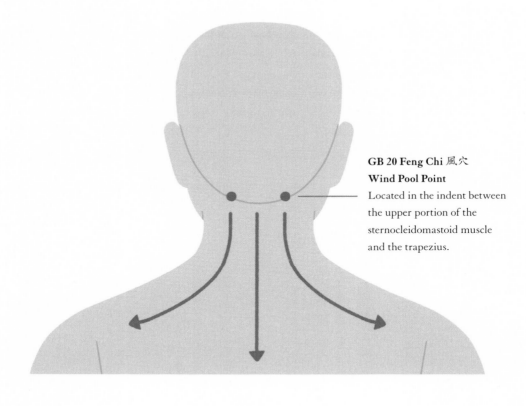

GB 20 Feng Chi 風穴
Wind Pool Point
Located in the indent between the upper portion of the sternocleidomastoid muscle and the trapezius.

Reflexology

- After 10 minutes of foot soaking, press below points on big toes for 10 to 15 minutes.

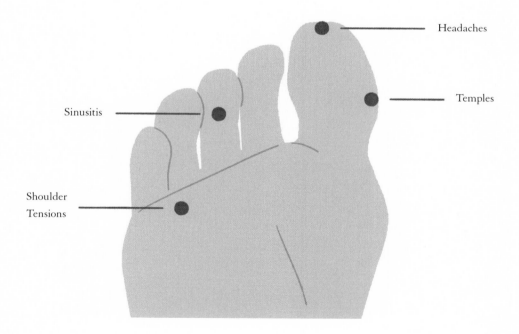

Every Cloud Has
a Silver Lining

Some good may come out of any
gloomy situation.
Always look for the silver lining, and
try to find the sunny side of life.

P.G. Wodehouse, 1920

Two months after I saw the movie of my life journey, I landed a teaching job in Mexico City. And despite strong opposition from my family, I left both my husband and Taiwan to start a new life in Mexico City with my children, with only fifty dollars in my pocket. Was I afraid? Yes, very much so. But I could no longer stay in my comfort zone because there was no more comfort zone anymore; I had to step out. I was sick of the familial arguments that repeated themselves over and over. I wanted a different life for myself and my children, for they were great kids and deserved a better life. I knew that raising three kids on my own in a strange new country would be a great challenge, but I was willing to bite the bullet and persevere. "Walk in the faith," I would tell myself.

The night we left Taiwan, we were on the freeway heading to the international airport. Out of nowhere, I saw a beautiful firework sparkling brilliantly in the night sky. I told the children to look out the window for the sight, but it had already vanished.

The kids asked, "Mom, where? We didn't see anything."

"Just wait a moment; maybe it will appear again," I replied. But there were no more fireworks. That's strange. Why would there be fireworks today? It's not a holiday or a festival. Maybe it was a sign of encouragement from higher beings? I wondered to myself and smiled.

I was in Mexico from age thirty-six to forty-two, and during those six years, I was fortunate to become the principal of a well-known Chinese school. I was delighted and enjoyed working in the education and culture field. Three years in a row, I successfully organized a big Chinese Festival parade held in front of tens of thousands of people.

While in Mexico, my sister gave me an acupuncture treatment every week, and I took TCM herbs daily to help with my depression. I also began to study Chinese medicine after work and every weekend. During that intensive year of working and learning, the love and support of my TCM classmates and friends in Mexico City slowly allowed me to heal and transition from Western antidepressants to herbal medicine.

Slowly I began my ascent out of the dark abyss of depression. The work in Mexico brought unprecedented achievements and confidence. My world was soon filled with light, color, and love once more, and those positive feelings rebuilt my health and happiness. That year I turned forty.

But there is good and bad to everything. With all the responsibilities, I had a hectic lifestyle with much emotional entanglement, so even though there was no more depression, other health issues began to occur. As my health faltered, gastric ulcers and esophagitis formed; the problems lasted for years until I finally went for a physical.

I was diagnosed with a precancerous condition called Barrett's esophagus with high-grade dyspepsia. Dysplasia is an early stage in cancer development, and the probability that it will turn into esophageal cancer was relatively high, about fifteen percent of cases per year. Cancer of the esophagus is deadly, so if left untreated, the odds were that I'd develop cancer within three to five years, use a Nasogastric tube for feeding, then die shortly afterward.

During the depression, it took me two years of fear and hesitation to finally step out of my comfort zone to make a change. This time, with cancer to face, I refused to be afraid and instead saw this as an opportunity for change sent from the higher beings.

After only a week of consideration, I decided to quit my job, leave Mexico, and move my family to the United States. There I became a full-time student of Oriental medicine and acupuncture and spent the next seven years working on a doctor's degree until I could eventually start my clinic.

I treated myself with acupuncture twice a week for my gastric ulcers and esophagus symptoms. I also watched what I ate. Coffee, apples, and lemon juice hurt my stomach during that period, so I quit eating those that were my favorite foods for over two years. It might be strange that I abstained from apples. But for me, during that time, acids hurt my digestive system. That's why I always mention to my patients: know your body, watch what you eat, everybody is unique, everybody is different, no one knows us better than ourselves.

To treat myself, I would insert needles in my toes and legs and lie down slowly. Then I would put needles on my abdominal region, head, and lastly, my hands. After around five minutes, I would feel my muscles and tendons collapse into a really calm, soft, relaxed, and peaceful state.

After each treatment, I always felt a lot of energy and peace inside me, and that made me say, "Thank you, our wise ancestors! It's an amazing healing technique, and I'm so lucky to be able to practice this healing method."

The first two years of attending Master of Oriental Medicine school, I would have stomach aches and mid-back pain halfway through the class; my face would turn pale, and I'd curl up in my seat. My professors and classmates all came to help.

One day, after two years of frequent needling treatment, my "Internal Diagnostic" course professor asked to check every student's pulse for training purposes. I was the last to be checked. The teacher then announced, with a surprised look on her face, "Unbelievable! Jessie now has the healthiest pulse in the class, healthier than each one of you."

Life in Los Angeles was simple and less stressful. I focused on my studies, and with the frequent treatment, my symptoms and pains went away. A few months later, I went back to Taiwan for another physical check-up to confirm my suspicion. The report came back clean: Barrett's esophagus had not progressed. It was stable, which was good news because that meant that I could maintain my health with natural TCM and acupuncture. I felt healed and reborn.

During that time, I filed for a divorce. I had an intense eagerness to regain my freedom and bravely embark on a journey of self-healing without the suppressing opposite force of a stressful relationship. I needed to end my twenty-five-year marriage. My children adapted quickly and loved the peaceful life in Los Angeles. I once more embarked on a journey of self-healing.

With this fifteen year-long journey of depression, I learned that we couldn't only focus on prayer faith. It's not only spiritual awareness that wins the battle: there are physical, emotional, and psychological issues at play as well. When the body is out of balance, it affects our emotional and mental states. Similarly, if our emotional and mental states are unwell, the body's meridian energy and blood flow may be blocked, thus causing sickness. All of the systems are interdependent.

Looking back, I know that according to TCM, depression and other mental disorders are mainly caused by an imbalance of the Heart meridian and organ systems, which cause depression and other mental illnesses (because the heart controls our mind, spirit, and the emotion of joy). And then, combined with secondary meridians and unbalanced organs -such as Spleen and Stomach, Kidney and Urination, Liver and Gallbladder, or Lung with Large Intestine- these dysfunctional can stack up to create major health problems.

It wasn't until after studying TCM doctor programs and learning of cosmic medicine that I found out each of us has a weak and strong aspect of our nature when we are born. For the year I was born, I was destined to have access to the heart's fire, which would also become the weak part of my health.

My PPD was caused by blood deficiency after multiple childbirths that significantly affected my heart. Along with a weakly functioning spleen and stomach system since childhood, these factors combined and triggered PPD. My health went downhill silently, without my noticing, while I was busy taking care of my babies. Then everything fell apart, and the severe depression occurred.

That's why, using nature and nurture, we have to put fifty percent of the effort into our body, keeping all the meridians, energy, blood, and nutrition in balance. And another fifty percent of the action on our emotions, mindset, and spirit. We have to know ourselves mentally and physically first. We must take care of ourselves first; then and only then can we start to take care of others.

Five elements chart - Organs, Seasons and Emotion Relationship

	Wood	Fire	Earth	Metal	Water
Yin Organ	Liver	Heart	Spleen	Lung	Kidney
Yang Organ	Gallbladder	Small intestine	Stomach	Large Intestine	Urinary Bladder
Taste	Sour	Bitter	Sweet	Pungent	Salty
Tissue	Tendons	Blood vessels	Muscles	Skin	Bones
Season	Spring	Summer	Late summer	Autumn	Winter
Positive Emotion	Strategic, decision making	Joyful, merciful	Thoughtful, accepting	Conducting positive energy	Wise, active
Negative Emotion	Angry, anxious	Grudging, pessimistic	Impatient, complaining	Sorrowful, regretful	Fearful, depressed

My favorite self-help tip for the stomach and abdominal pain

For releasing sharp pain of the stomach region
- Press on ST34 Liang Qiu 梁丘 and RN12 Zhong Wan 中脘 points for 15 seconds and release for 5 seconds; repeat as needed. Usually, it takes a few minutes to release the pain.
- Put a heating mat on the abdominal region.

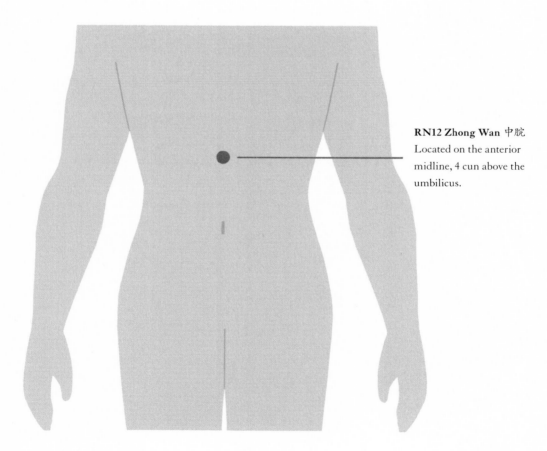

RN12 Zhong Wan 中脘
Located on the anterior midline, 4 cun above the umbilicus.

RN12 Zhong Wan 中脘

Use this point for:
- Stomachache, abdominal distension, indigestion.
- Nausea, vomiting.
- Heartburn, diarrhea.

ST34 Liang Qiu 梁丘

Use this point for:
- Acute stomach pain, gastric pain, mastitis, GERD, vomiting.
- Knee pain and swelling, difficulty movement of pain region.

ST36 Zu San Li 足三里穴

Use this point for:
- Chronic illness.
- Stomach issues.
- Poor digestion.
- Psychological, emotional disorders like PMS, depression, anxiety, and insomnia.
- Low immunity.
- Building and maintaining overall health.

ST34 Liang Qiu 梁丘
Located above the knee, two cun above the superior lateral, on the border of the patella.

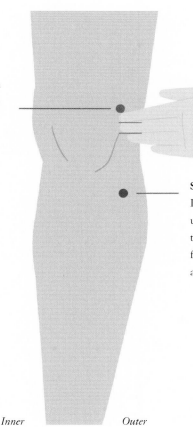

ST36 Zu San Li 足三里穴
Located on the outside of the leg under the knee, three cun below the knee indentation, and one finger width lateral from the tibia's anterior border.

Inner   *Outer*

The Younger,
The Active.
The Older,
The Wiser

Fresh ginger as army vanguard, old ginger as national guard.

Dr. Jessie Lee

When my three children came to Mexico City with me in 2008, they were fifteen, ten, and six years old. When visiting Mexico, it is paramount to visit the UNESCO Intangible Cultural Heritage of Humanity: The Pyramid of Teotihuacan, or "the place where gods are created," the largest city in ancient Mesoamerica, near present-day Mexico City: site of extensive archaeological ruins. Mexico City is located at an altitude of 3930 meters high (12,890 feet), and the climate is cool and pleasant.

It was July, a beautiful summer day. We chose a holiday for this day trip with my sister's family and several of the Chinese school staff members. Because we were a group of Chinese living overseas, the China embassy always looked out for us. I remember two days before the trip, I received a phone call from the Education Counselor from the embassy.

The counselor caller asked, "Are you planning on visiting the pyramids this week?"

"Yes! We have a holiday!" I replied happily.

"No, I mean, even though it's summer, July is the rainy season In Mexico. You might get caught in a rainstorm, and it could be dangerous," the caller said.

"I appreciate your concern, but I think we'll be just fine," I said. "Don't worry, thank you again." Hanging up the phone, I mumbled to myself, "The weather is beautiful now, we'll be fine."

On the day of the trip, everyone was excited. After driving about an hour outside of the city, we saw plains full of wild cacti taller than people. A little further out, we were suddenly able to see the tips of the pyramids appearing on the horizon. Everyone in the car was buzzing with excitement, the children started to dance and sing in the car. The view of the ancient pyramids standing sturdily in the field was truly a magnificent sight.

When we arrived at the parking area, it was almost lunchtime so we decided to fill our empty bellies and replenish our energy before climbing the pyramid. After eating lunch, the sky was blue, with only a few white clouds in sight. It seemed like a good time for us to head for the pyramids. By the time we arrived at the huge square in front of the pyramid, threatening clouds had started to gather. We didn't pay it much attention, for we were all too excited. We began to climb, and the steps were about two and a half times taller than standard stairs, so the effort required to reach the top slowed us down considerably.

At this point, the dark clouds above had covered the sky completely and appeared quite ominous. But I was optimistic and thought, that's good, the clouds are blocking the sun and keeping us cool.

Everyone was on their hands and feet, crawling up slowly step by step. The rain started to drizzle, but it didn't matter! When we were about two-thirds of the way up, it began raining harder, with small chunks of hail falling out of the sky. The crowd around us began to speed up the climb. We struggled to keep up, and about five minutes later, we set foot on top of the pyramid.

Suddenly a blast of thunder startled everyone. I looked up, and it was as if someone had punched a massive hole in the sky: the temperature dropped sharply, and the rain and hail began to pour. Everyone was frightened and stunned; somewhere to the right, we heard screams and children crying. We just stood in place, soaking wet and trying to protect our heads from the hail with our hands.

Finally, the adults snapped out of it. We gathered the children to the middle and urged everyone to climb down. It was freezing. My whole body was trembling involuntarily, and the children in my arms began to cry with fear.

"Don't be afraid, and It will pass soon," I tried comforting them through trembling teeth. I began to think, "Oh my God! I'm freezing to death! My heart can't stand it, and my limbs are numb."

Then miraculously, the thunderstorm stopped. It was gone just as suddenly as it had appeared. The sky no longer roared, and only a gentle sprinkle of rain continued. But we still had a way to go from the top of the pyramid. It took about twenty minutes to return to the ground safely.

Soaked to the bones, we rushed to the car without stopping and blasted the heater as soon as we all got in. There was no way to change out of wet clothes. The kids began to sneeze, and my head began to throb. I immediately thought of ginger tea. I picked up the phone and called my mom. Fortunately, my mother had not come to the pyramids with us that day and had stayed at home instead.

I told her, "Mom! Hurry, cook a big pot of ginger tea with some brown sugar for twelve people. We got caught in a thunderstorm while on top of the pyramid. Everyone is soaked and freezing. We will be home in about half an hour."

When we got home and rushed into the house, Mom handed the ginger tea to everyone. The children didn't complain as they usually did, crying out, "Spicy! Too hot!" Instead, they complied and drank the warm sweet tea. Immediately we felt a warm energy flow through our bodies, and we were no longer cold. After that, everyone quickly went for hot baths and changed out of wet clothes.

Fresh ginger tea plays a role in dispelling the invasion of external factors, which are cold and dampness. No one in our group of twelve got sick from the trip that day, and it was an unforgettable experience. The children also learned that ginger tea is a valuable natural remedy for colds.

Ginger tea for cold

200 ml of hot water + 1 tbsp. of grated ginger

Leave to infuse for ten minutes, then add honey and a slice of lemon.

Ginger for removing headache

Cook slices of ginger and apply on the forehead when it's warm, for 10 to 15 minutes, then reheat when ginger slices get cold.

Ginger may irritate some skin types. For pregnant and breastfeeding women and those with bleeding disorders, diabetes, and heart conditions, please take extra care and consult with your physician first.

Note: For TCM/OM, we have to distinguish between external wind-cold or external wind-heat because we treated it with different herbs depending on the body type. Discuss with your TCM doctor to know more about your body type.

Antennas On The Head

Scalp acupuncture is like Neuroacupuncture; the needles are inserted into loose tissue layers of the scalp to stimulate, to waken, and promote the brain neurons, to help problems such as strokes, paralysis, dementia, insomnia, anxiety and more.

Dr. Jessie Lee

When my mother was seventy-four years old, my only brother was shot and killed during a robbery in Honduras, Central America. This sudden and terrible news shocked us all. I was distraught that my mother couldn't handle this blow, so I watched her closely.

Mother is a faithful Christian, and she knew that God would take care of everything and that everything happens for a reason, so for the first six months, she was able to hold onto her faith by a thread. We were all delighted that she was able to find comfort in God during this dark time.

But because her logic suppressed her emotions, she did not allow herself to be appropriately sad; her feelings became extreme and affected her psychological state. She became depressed and started to have mood disorders (in the psychology field; they call it Delayed Onset Post traumatic Stress Disorder - DSM-IV American Psychiatry Association).

Six months after my brother's funeral, my formerly healthy and happy mother began to feel very sick. She felt tremendous body pain and suffocation during specific times of the evening every day. There is a term 'sundowner' in the care giving field. From TCM's perspective, 5:00 PM to 7:00 PM is the time for the kidney meridians and system to recharge their energy (like a circadian rhythm). Therefore, if the kidney system is weak, and the kidneys store the fear emotion, one will feel even more uncomfortable and fearful for no reason during the evening. Many older adults have a deficiency in essential kidney energy, and that is how I began understanding how the sundowner syndrome came about.

According to TCM, the kidneys manage our 'fear' emotion; if we feel fear often, that negative energy will attack our kidney function. On the contrary, people born with weak kidneys or those who have had their kidneys go wrong for some reason may experience unreasonable fear easily.

My brother's death made my mom feel unsafe, insecure, and afraid about life, and that fear crippled her body's health very quickly. Every day she would shout,

"I can't breathe! Call an ambulance and take me to the ER! There's a problem with my heart!"

Or she would say, "I have a stomachache, something stuck. I can't walk because of the pressure, it may be a tumor, take me to the hospital."

Or, "I can't eat because my stomach is bloated, I have to go to the hospital to check."

Or, "I can't sleep. I toss and turn all night. Take me to the hospital."

Or, "I can't go to the bathroom, my stomach is in pain now, take me to the hospital..."

In sunny California, she woke up every morning, saw the bright sunshine, then said in a melancholy tone, "It's a sunny day, too bright, too hot at noon."

Finally came a cloudy day. I said happily, "Wow! Finally, today is cloudy. It won't be so bright and hot. Isn't that nice?"

She said, "Oh! Is it cloudy? Then wait a minute, will it be too cold for me? What should I do?"

It's depression – the inability to see the positive. I quickly diagnosed my mom's symptoms as depression, but she disagreed and said, "I don't think depression would cause me to hurt everywhere on my body! It must be pain caused by a tumor."

So began her four-year journey to restore her health. Every two months, she went to a different country to have health checks and get some treatments. She went to Germany with my elder sister and let herself be checked and treated, but after two months, Mom began quarreling to leave. She flew back to Taiwan with my aunts and went to have a complete health check, and reported that her results were normal. Mom didn't believe it, got annoyed, and flew back to the United States to let me treat her. After two months, she went for an examination and treatment in my second sister's Chinese medicine hospital in Mexico.

In this way, four years went by, my mother traveled continuously among the four different countries, receiving Western and Eastern medicine, trying all sorts of therapies to ease her suffering. When my mother was sick during the five long years, I tried everything I knew to treat her. But maybe my skills weren't mature enough, or perhaps it wasn't the time yet, but I was only able to barely keep her from falling off the edge while she gradually worsened every day. When her appetite grew low and her metabolism slowed down, her body became even weaker.

Finally, there was a day she went out to the neighbor's house, just across the street, to borrow some salt for cooking. Then she forgot the way back home! Lost, she wandered around in the community for almost twenty minutes before returning to my neighbor's door and asking anxiously,

"Can you show me how to get back home? I can't find the way back."

Our neighbor kindly walked her back home, I realized, Oh my God, Mom has symptoms of dementia.

Mom also developed a strange behavior: she became like a detective. She didn't read books, watch TV, or play the piano like she used to; she lost interest in everything. But she would walk noiselessly like our cats and stand silently behind everyone in the house to watch what they were doing. Often we would get shocked and jump because Mom would suddenly sneak up from behind like a ghost.

She also began forgetting things she had experienced before. For example, she pointed to a chair in the living room and asked, "What is that?"

"A massage chair that I gave you as a Mother's Day gift last year," I replied.

"No, I never saw that chair before. Let me try; it looks interesting."

I made jokes to my children and said, "This is quite good. If I ever forget like that, every day after a night's sleep is like a brand new slate. I would experience everything like it is all new."

Once the time was ripe, crystal healing and cranial scalp needling techniques came to the rescue.

I put needles on my mom's scalp every night before she went to bed while she slept on an amethyst-infused heating mat, on top of her head where mom would not touch the needles if she tossed and turned in her sleep. The needles were left in until I took them out before going to bed myself, and she would continue to sleep undisturbed.

Unexpectedly, after a week of continuous scalp acupuncture, we all noticed a good improvement. It was so effective, and I continued the treatments for three months to get mom back to normal.

The four needles placed on the top of Mom's head looked just like four antennas. The children noticed their grandma's progress and remarked that they didn't expect that installing antennas on top of Grandma's head would work so well. After seeing the results, I decided to try this on myself. During the three months of preparing for my license exam, I 'installed' the four antennas on my head before studying and felt that enhanced my concentration. I was able to read faster and memorize better. I have to thank the ancient sages for blessing the world with the knowledge of these antennas that successfully helped me achieve my acupuncture license.

When I went to Germany to visit my elder sister, I observed and assisted at her clinic every day. I helped to clean up, make beds, and to prepare tea for patients. Once, I saw a tall German policeman leaving the clinic with four antennas on his head. I quickly told my sister,

"There are still four needles on his head!"

"Yeah! I left it in because he still has to study tonight," she replied. "He is very nervous about his police advancement exam. Those four needles will not only help him calm down but will also increase his concentration and memory, so he will take them out on his own at home after studying." In Asia, it is common for acupuncturists to let patients go home with needles inserted, according to the needs of their conditions, with a good explanation of self-care at home.

My favorite self-help tip to stimulate the brain cortex

- Use ten fingers or a wooden hair comb to gently comb the scalp to stimulate Qi for ten to fifteen minutes a day. It refreshes the mind, enhances memory, and also promotes hair growth.

Si Shen Cong 四神聰穴 are acupuncture points for memory improvement, insomnia, dementia and peace of mind. It is placed on the top of the head at the intersection of the midline of the head, and the line of the tip of the ears. The four points of Si Shen Cong are one cun apart in each direction from DU20 Bai Hui 百會穴.

Si Shen Cong 四神聰穴

DU20 **Bai Hui** 百會穴

Hey,
Is That Abuse?

A person with a long-time illness will
become a good doctor.

Proverb from Ancient China

In 2014, we had six cats at home in Los Angeles. On a rare quiet day when no one was home, I decided to bathe them one by one, bending over the outer ridge of the bathtub to wash them so they wouldn't escape.

After an hour and a half, I finished cleaning all six cats, and I tried to stand up straight.

OUCH! A sharp pain shot up my lower back, and the slightest movement would send fresh waves of pain. I was stuck. What do I do? I couldn't call for help because I was home alone.

Suddenly, I remembered what I've learned from the acupuncture anatomy class from school: the lower back connected with the latissimus dorsi muscle. It would be difficult to insert needles on my lower back by myself, and I didn't have any needles by my side. Still, with the gua sha technique, I could easily access the area by just scraping my arm and low back with a rounded edge cup and baby oil.

It was the right spot. When I pressed those muscles, I felt a dull ache. The redness and bruising emerged very quickly to the skin's surface. Once the petechiae and ecchymosis, which we called "sha" appeared, immediately the pain lessened. I could stand up straight once more. I've used the guasha technique to loosen the tightened latissimus dorsi muscle.

I was happy that I could unstick myself from a sticky situation with such a simple technique. I started to use guasha frequently during my college life since I often had shoulder, arm, and back pain, plus headaches because I'd stay up late for design projects. I would scrape skin for a few minutes until the purple-red "sha" appeared, and then the pain was immediately relieved. I helped myself, and then my friends, to heal the pain.

I like to refer to guasha as the "clean window method" due to its works. Each capillary pore in the skin is just like a window of the body to communicate from the inside out; that's why we have to clean the body's windows to ensure continual communication.

One time during my Oriental Medicine clinical internship, I saw my Korean professor standing in the corridor, checking a patient's file with an exhausted face. I asked with concern:

"Doctor, are you OK? You look so tired and pale."

He replied, "I have a headache and shoulder pains. Might have caught a cold..."

"Would you like me to put some needles in you to help release the pain?"

"Nope, we have many patients waiting right now, no time to treat me."

"Let me think of a simple way to treat you...Why don't you let me do gua sha on your neck and shoulder now? It just takes a few minutes, and at least you would feel better for a while."

The doctor accepted my suggestion, "Okay, I'll let you do that."

I took out my gua sha cream from my white gown (I always carry that tool with me), I applied the cream on the skin of his neck and shoulder and then scraped. With only three short scrapes, the 'sha' came out a lot, so I finished scraping the neck and shoulder region within just three minutes.

"I feel refreshed, and the pain has reduced to almost nothing now," my professor said with a surprised voice. "Thank you very much. You have excellent scraping skills, which I don't often see among students who use this technique. Maybe you can help me do gua sha after clinic hours?"

"Sure! My pleasure!" I replied happily.

Because the scraping result was so good for my professor, I won the "SoHo" scraper title among our student members. But in the U.S, when my Caucasian friends saw the bruising on my arm, they were often shocked and worried.

"Did someone hurt you? What happened to your arm? Do you need help? Do we need to call the police?" They would ask frantically.

I often have to explain to people about gua sha therapy. People tend to get scared because of how the bruising looks. This natural therapy intentionally raises transitory therapeutic extravasated blood in the subcutis, represented by petechiae, and could be resolved in two to four days.

Gua sha has been shown to be effective in randomized trials for pain management; it helps for acute and chronic pains, headaches, migraines, shoulder, arm, lower back, joint pains, influenza, and more. It's easy to get a heat stroke during the summer, and the muggy hot weather often causes headaches, dizziness, nausea, pain, and stiffness in the neck and back. Gua sha is particularly useful in helping heatstroke, also suitable for stiffness and aches caused by sitting in front of a computer for too long.

Healers in ancient Asia used smooth-edged stones, bones, and bamboo to perform guasha. Most mothers and grandmothers in my homeland culture use a glass or ceramic soup spoon to gently scrape the skin, much like giving a deep tissue massage; applied oil or water to the skin before scraping. Once the bruising come up to the skin's surface, the stiffness and pain go away. That's why it's also known as "Grandma's therapy."

Gua sha therapy works by scraping the troubled area's skin to release muscle tension and loosen the muscles, thus reducing the pain. Gua sha is a technique mostly accessible to everyone and can easily be done by oneself.

Now, I'm going to pick up a cup and scrape my shoulder to relieve the soreness caused by typing on a computer for too long.

Guasha Therapy Directions

Back

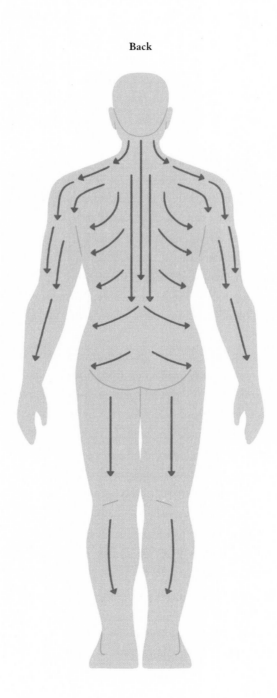

Guasha Therapy Tools

Use tools with round and smooth edges, such as ceramic cups and spoons, coins, and guasha stone. Make sure to clean the tools before and after use.

Guasha Stone

Coin

Ceramic Spoon

Ceramic Cup

Note
- *Those currently taking anticoagulant medication, NSAIDs, Vitamin E, or fish oils, or bleeding disorders should be cautious of receiving gua sha treatments. Consult your practitioner first.*
- *Gua sha may cause petechiae where applied. This ecchymosis could be resolved in two to four days.*
- *One should keep the Gua sha treatment area protected from wind, cold, and water drafts within thirty minutes to an hour after performing the method.*

Pepperoni Marks, Cupping, Healing

Only one treatment may not solve the problem, but it can change your mind. What life can't give you, love can! Believe in your instinct, because that inspiration comes from Divine guidance; and then we will know what's best and that it will work out well.

Dr. Jessie Lee

One day during clinical practice at the Oriental Medicine school, there came a patient with a chief complaint of lower back pain for the past half-year, with a pain level of eight out of ten. But what called my attention to his case was what I saw in his medical history. He had third stage liver cancer, had undergone surgery and ten rounds of chemotherapy in the previous six months, and was convalescing at home without taking any medicine.

The patient's pulse was tight and wiry, and his tongue was reddish purple and dry without coating. That was the first time I had seen it in clinical practice. I saw that type of tongue picture shown in the textbook only. School has taught me that most patients get this kind of tongue after chemotherapy or long term illness, like ten or twenty years of taking medication. We call it Ying deficiency in Oriental Medicine terms; it also brings inner heat, irritability, and frustration.

The first two treatment sessions I worked on balancing his twelve meridians, and the moving Qi needle technique to adjust his Yin and Yang to release pain. I imagined that he would return to the clinic and tell me, "Very effective! The pain gradually slowed down, and I slept better" as it usually happened for other lower back pain patients.

But it surprised me when he arrived limping back with his wife's help. He said, "There is not much improvement. I was fine for only one day, and then the pain came back. Doctor, why does it work only for one day?"

Hmm, good question. After thinking to myself a minute, I explained, "Usually, the efficacy of acupuncture is up to seventy-two hours and sometimes longer, but in your case, it was less. Imagine that each of the small cells in our body is like a little person living among others in one social environment, busy communicating.

"I used to live in many other countries and cities with heavy and chaotic traffic systems. Those congested urban routes are like a body with a low immune system, weak and sick. But in some countries, people are more law-abiding and disciplined like we are now in the United States. Even when an accident happens and traffic occurs but quickly returns to normal after the police come to give orders and clear things up.

"Acupuncture needles are like the police that give orders to our cell communities. They try make people more disciplined. In the beginning, you can rely on the frequent police patrol (more intensive treatment) to train the body, but you still have to return to the consciousness of balance. That is the ultimate way to retain health."

He nodded and said: "Understood, Doctor! I need to train my cells to be back in the balanced state."

Suddenly, a thought came to my mind; I decided to use fire-cupping therapy on him.

I explained to him the details of what cupping does and the "pepperoni marks" they leave. Fire-cupping is good to clear creating, open muscle tightness and stagnation, and eliminate swelling and pain. That's why so many athletes like to use this therapy to help them release their muscle soreness.

A good and patient explanation invariably soothes the patient's fear. He agreed to try cupping. I applied the cups to his back and legs.

After treatment, he bent himself easily and naturally to put his shoes on. Elated, he exclaimed, "Look at me! I can now bend down easily to adjust my shoes!"

His wife was astonished and said, "But you were always able to do it yourself."

He replied, "No! I had a hard time bending over after surgery, and it has been tough for me to put on shoes since."

"Why didn't you let me know this? You should have told me." quipped his wife with a distressed expression.

"I did not want you to worry." he said.

I was deeply moved by their intimate conversation. How brave the husband was! He was so uncomfortable with all the pain in his body caused by cancer, but he didn't complain; he bore his severe pain in silence and pretended that everything was fine to keep his family from worrying.

Finally, this cupping therapy was successfully effective! For his next appointment, he walked in lightly by himself into the examination room and told me that he had no back pain for the past four days and that his sleep quality had improved.

Cupping and needles alleviated the patient's lower back pain symptoms after six visits in three weeks. He could extend the time between clinic visits and let his body gradually resume its normal operations. Ten sessions is always the best way to meet one complete round of treatment.

Note

- *Those currently taking anticoagulant medication, NSAIDs, Vitamin E, or fish oils, or bleeding disorders should be cautious of receiving gua sha treatments. Consult your practitioner first.*
- *Cupping may leave red or bruise-like circular marks where the cups are applied. These marks are common with this technique, and could be resolved in two to four days.*
- *One should keep the cupped area protected from wind, cold, and water drafts within thirty minutes to an hour after cupping.*
- *Cupping is useful for cold dampness, dredging the meridians, dispelling stasis, promoting qi and blood circulation, expelling swelling and pain, clearing heat, and adjusting the body to keep in balance.*

Cupping marks and what they mean

Slight Pink

Good circulation

Blisters

Excess dampness

Bright Red

Inner heat

Dark Purple

Bad circulation

Paleness

Chi deficiency, weakness

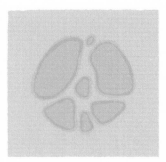

Rash

Chi deficiency

I Will Fix You

死馬當活馬醫 (si ma dang huo ma yi)
To treat a dead horse as if it is alive.

Chinese Proverb from Song Dynasty
AC.960-1279

It means to keep trying everything in a
desperate situation. Make a last attempt
to save a hopeless case, a hopelessly
optimistic try.

Xun Xun is a three-year-old Siamese gentleman cat we brought to the United States from Mexico in 2011. Even though he was an outdoor cat, he would always come home to sleep and eat every night. But once, he disappeared for three days and didn't come home. I was worried sick; every night before I went to bed, I called his name at the door wishing him back home soon. One night around eleven o'clock, I went downstairs to the door calling his name and checked if I locked the door before
going to bed. I heard a weak meow by the corner of the glass door. It was Xun Xun!

I called out, "Xun Xun, is that you? You're back!"

I was so happy and relieved.

But something was wrong. Xun Xun didn't hop inside immediately like he usually did. Instead, he just crouched there and meowed at me weakly, appearing very tired. I took a closer look at him and realized that his shoulder was bleeding and he couldn't move at all.

"What happened to you?" I cried out.

I brought him into the house. Upon closer inspection, I found that he had also injured his spine, which caused his paralysis. He was unable to stand, walk, or relieve himself properly. He barely managed to crawl back home using his two front legs. I don't know how long he had crawled, but I knew that he must have suffered a lot. He looked frail, filthy, and close to dying.

It was late at night and the animal hospital had already closed, so I applied some Chinese herbal powder onto his wound and laid him down in a quiet corner of the house. The next day, I found his injury improved a lot better, so I nursed his wound twice a day, cleaned his excrement, and watched him like a hawk, trying to keep him in a sanitary state. His eyes were full of sorrow whenever he had a bowel movement or urinated. Cats love to be clean, but he couldn't control it.

After five days of treatment with Chinese herbal powder, his terrible wound healed and I took him to the vet. The x-ray showed a fracture in his tailbone and a dislocation in his spinal area. The estimated surgery cost came out to around four to five thousand dollars, with a fifty percent chance of success. If it failed, Xun Xun could be paralyzed for the rest of his life, and we'd better put him down to stop suffering. That was cruel, terrible news. The animal spinal surgery was costly to me; Without a steady income I was already in debt for my studies and, not to mention the risky surgery. But I didn't want to give up.

I thought, "Acupuncture works for humans. I believe it'll work in this situation too. Let me help Xun Xun with tiny needles."

So I took him back home before I called and consulted my nephew who is a veterinarian in Taiwan; veterinarian hospital often uses acupuncture remedies for animals. My nephew sent me a cat acupoint chart. I followed the indication for spinal injury. I put needles on both sides of the vertebral spinal area to the tailbone region. Xun Xun sensed that I, as his mom, was trying to help him, so he cooperated, staying still while letting me put the tiny needles into him every day.

I had to wash him of defecation before leaving in needles for thirty minutes. Hence, it took me almost an hour and a half to treat Xun Xun in a session. I also took him to my upperclassmen doctor Stephen Yan, who helped me check my cat son and used Tui Na's massage on Xun Xun and taught me to continue doing the Tui Na to him. I was very appreciative of Dr. Yan's willingness to help.

Finally, on the fortieth day, Xun Xun could stand up little by little despite some difficulty. His first steps were going to the litter box and relieving himself. I saw his smile, and tears of filled my eyes.

I witnessed my father treating himself successfully with acupuncture for his paralysis twice, that inspired me to keep trying too. Xun Xun recovered ninety five percent with only a mild imbalance on his hip, but otherwise resumed normal daily activities till he was ten years old.

Neck

If the upper beam is not straight, the lower ones will go aslant. A crooked stick will have a crooked shadow.

Chinese Proverb

When I came home from work one day, my youngest son came to me with an injured nose that was bruised and swollen.

"Wow, what happened to your nose?" I asked.

"I fell and hit my face on the living room floor," he replied.

"What? How did that happen?"

"I don't know, I was sitting in the chair doing my homework for almost two hours without getting up. Then the cats were meowing at me to let them out. So I stood up to open the door. Then I felt dizzy and my vision faded. I blacked out and fell to the ground. When I woke up, I found myself face down on the floor, and my nose was all bruised up and swollen."

"Hmmm… maybe you stood up too fast, but let me check your neck. Go lie down on the treatment table."

Immediately I found his second and third cervical spine mildly dislocated toward the right side neck. As we know, those spinal dislocations may cause a host of symptoms such as a stuffy nose, allergies, tinnitus, earache, dizziness, blindness, nerve pains, and acne. I also found his ninth thoracic vertebra mildly misaligned toward the left side. It's the compensatory effect. And said, "If the upper beam is not straight, the lower ones will go aslant."

I explained to him, "Because you sat for so long with such bad posture, your neck muscles turned stiff and pulled the spine off-center, which pressed on the nerves. Then you stood up suddenly and experienced dizziness, blindness and collapsed."

When we look down for a long time and stress our neck muscles, vertebra dislocation could happen by improper posture, especially in modern days of often using smartphones and operating computers. People often get cervical dislocation from this, which then causes internal problems and body aches. Sometimes, external factor invasions can also be generated, such as wind, cold, heat, dampness, dryness, food poisoning, and emotional stress. All these external factors cause tightness in the muscles and tendons, then pull the spine off course.

One day, a young twenty-one year old patient came to me with constant severe left-side migraines and blurred vision that she had been experiencing for around six weeks. She had gone to her primary doctor, and they had arranged an MRI for her since they thought it might be a brain tumor causing her symptoms. But the doctor set the MRI appointment for one month in the future, and the migraines were causing her so much suffering and lousy vision that she decided to come to me first.

I checked her pulse first. It showed that her liver meridian had high pressure, and her lung system had an external factor invasion. I immediately knew that she had a cold and was stressed by cervical dislocation. According to TCM, our liver system controls the eye and vision functions. Next, I checked her neck and cervical spinal system.

"Bingo!" I said. "Your axis cervical are mildly displaced towards the right side. Does it hurt when I press on this area?"

I added some pressure with my fingertips and she winced.

"This type of dislocation causes dizziness, acne, headaches, migraines... Don't worry, let me put some needles to release neck tension, and also to regulate your liver, lung, and spleen meridians; it should help with your migraine and blurry vision."

After only forty minutes of treatment, her migraine stopped and her vision improved. She stood up and gave me a big hug.

"It feels like I just woke up from a long sleep," she told me. "With the blurry vision and migraines, it felt as if I were trapped in a terrible nightmare."

From my own experience, my skin allergies and sinusitis started when I was sixteen years old. Most of the time, I couldn't smell anything, and I sneezed a lot. Thirty years later, when I was forty-six, my sister Dr. Mei, who is a spinal specialist acupuncturist, checked my spine. She found that I have severe cervical spondylosis, and used her skill to help adjust my cervical problems when I visited her in Mexico.

Back in the US, my friends Dr. Chang and his wife Grace used OPT therapy, and continued treating my occipital and cervical region once a week for six weeks, and I wrap a heating pad on my neck every day for an hour while using the computer in those treatment session time frames; the heating pad helps for better circulation and softens the stiffness. Finally, my thirty years of sinus symptoms went away, and I can smell normally again. What a blessing! Now, I know I have to keep a lookout on my posture while working or sitting to keep my spine from dislocating again. Chiropractors are also helpful and useful to help adjust the spinal vertebra dislocation issue. We acupuncturists often work with the chiropractor to better support the patients.

1. *OPT Therapy English version can find in here: http://cch-foundation.org/content/?2715.html*

My favorite self-help tip for taking care of the cervical spine

- Keep an eye on the posture of the neck. Avoid bending the neck downwards or hunching forward for prolonged periods of time.
- When working, sitting, or reading, take a break every thirty minutes, and stretch in six directions: head down, head up, flexing left and right, turning head left and right, and stay still for ten to fifteen seconds each time.
- Place a heating mat on the neck to help the muscle maintain softness and for better circulation.
- Be aware of what you eat. The Stomach, Gallbladder, Urinary, and Triple-Warmer meridians go through the back of the neck; If something stresses the digestion system, it may trigger neck stiffness and pain.

It's Moxa,
Not Marijuana

"Curing Winter Diseases in the Summer."
It also cures summer diseases in the
winter using moxibustion remedy.

Indicated in ancient Chinese medical books.

My daughter recently graduated from college and started a new job in Portland, Oregon. It's a much colder state compared to ever-sunny California. Perhaps it was because of stress from work, a change in diet, or the cold and humid weather, but after three months, she came back home and asked me to check her pulse.

"Mom, check!" She held out her wrists. "What am I doing wrong? I've been losing a lot of hair in the past two weeks, are there any herbs I can take?"

Generally, it is normal to lose about a hundred strands of hair every day. However, if a large amount of hair loss occurs, it is necessary to find out what is off balance. After checking her pulse, I immediately detected an imbalance in her spleen and liver meridians. According to TCM theory, the spleen system produces blood while the liver restores it. Another belief is that "the hair is the material of blood," which means the hair is born of blood. If the body has enough blood, the hair will be abundant; if blood is insufficient, it will lose hair. My daughter's spleen function became weak, so the liver meridian experienced a blood deficiency, and as a result, she began to lose a lot of hair.

This time, I didn't need to deploy my army of needles. Instead, I instructed her to perform moxibustion twice a week, thirty minutes per session on specific points, until the heat penetrated and reddened the skin. While she was doing moxibustion, the smoke was so thick and strong it would fill the house. I reminded her to open the windows, since one time the fire alarm rang when I performed moxa at home. It gave everyone a bad scare. We all hurried to open the windows and turn on the ventilator; meanwhile, our neighbor walked by, smelled the strange smoke, and had a suspicious look on his face.

I explained, "Nothing happened. Everything is just fine. It's an herbal medicine called Asiatic Wormwood burned for treatment."

He chuckled and said, "Oh, I see. I thought it was marijuana."

My daughter didn't find the smoke from moxa bothersome. Instead, she found it warm, interesting and preferred it over needles. She did moxibustion twice a week, along with taking herbal supplements every day. After a week, I asked her:

"Do you think your hair is falling out less?" I asked.

"Yeah! It helped. I like moxa and herbal tea too," she replied.

As a child, I always loved watching my father perform moxibustion. He would use his hand to make cones of moxa herbs, place the cones atop slices of ginger, and then put it on a patient's knee. After completing the therapy, the patient would always exclaim, "The pain is relieved; my knee feels so much better now!"

TCM believes " Human body-Universe Interrelation Synchronize." A particular moxa therapy uses herbal patches put on the specific meridian points in the hottest and coldest season of the year.

It would stimulate the vibrant Yang Qi and blood circulation of the body, thereby adjusting organ function, improving the immune system, providing better body and mind tolerance, and boosting body resistance in the scorching and chilling period. It is a good way to achieve the best results for chronic respiratory diseases, asthma, allergic rhinitis, arthritis, low immunity, etc.

The hottest time of the year in the Northern Hemisphere is between July and August that starts on the summer solstice, known as Sanfu Tie (Sanfu-Moxibustion). The coolest time begins on the winter solstice and is known as Sanjiu Tie (Sanjiu- Moxibustion), which is the prime period for moxa treatments three to six times a year and repeatedly for three years. Because there are perennial roots to many diseases; patients of such conditions are susceptible to repeated recurrence; those chronic problems become severe when an alteration of climate occurs. That's what we called "Curing winter diseases in the summer and curing summer diseases in the winter", inherited from the ancient medical books.

I tried the moxa patch method on myself and also on my children. Another way of moxa therapy is cover the body with a bath towel, lay down a layer of grated ginger as base layer, then burn moxa herbs on top. Letting the herbal steam penetrate to the body for thirty minutes. We nicknamed it "Herbal Spa," and "Body BBQ."

As I have learned Shamanism's sage smoke therapy to cleanse one's space and energies to achieve a peaceful state, I found a similar healing function with moxibustion therapy. According to the thousand-year-old historical records, people used Artemisia/ Asiatic Wormwood smoke to cleanse the air during a pandemic outbreak in ancient times. There is a ritual of hanging a bundle of dry Artemisia/ Asiatic Wormwood on the front door to prevent the season's negative energies, ending on Dragon Boat Festival day.

One day I saw the movie "The Two Popes", and I was amazed by the smoke ritual they performed in the Catholic church. What a coincidence! It is an intriguing field of study that requires further research.

Herbal AcuPatch

This is an excellent option for non-needle support, for use against respiratory disease, rheumatic disease, digestive problems, or weakend immune system.

Sanfu Tie 三伏貼 (Sanfu-Moxibustion), place on the points in the hottest time in a year.
Sanjiu Tie 三九貼 (Sanjiu- Moxibustion), place on the points in the coolest time in a year.

1. Mix water and ground herbs.
2. Apply on points.
3. Cover with acupatch to hold in place.
4. Leave for 30 minutes, then remove the patch and wipe off herb residue with water.

Moxa and Ginger Combination

1. Get a thin slice of ginger.
2. Poke holes in the slice of ginger.
3. Arrange moxa in a cone shape then place on top of ginger.
4. Apply on points.

Note: Consult with your TCM doctor for perscribed points.

Be careful not to burn the skin.
Remove moxa when it becomes too hot.

Moxa Stick

Hover above skin in a clock-wise
motion for five to ten minutes until
the skin turns slightly red.

Important -
Put moxa in a glass jar, then close tightly after use to ensure it is
completely extinguished.

Magic Holographic Therapy

Every dust mote contains
three thousand worlds.

Buddha

The holographic theory of TCM originates from the Yellow Emperor's Canon of Internal Medicine. The book explores the holographic principle related to the human body and then applies this insight to guide the clinical practice. Chinese medicine believes that the human body's five senses (eyes, ears, nose, tongue, and skin) are portals to the human body's five internal organs, leading to its surface. Observing the color of the body parts also helps to diagnose the patient.

I have learned from 'Lingshu' (Spiritual Pivot), which is quoted, "the kidney is in the ear...The eyes are the portal of the liver." Another example is Zhang Zhongjing's A Medical Saint in Han Dynasty (A.C. 150-219) which states that "when the nose is green it means the stomach is cold; when the nose is red it means the stomach has excess heat." These texts help us diagnose and show the way of the wisdom of the holographic theory.

Theres a saying from Buddha before 2500 B.C.E., "Every mote of dust contains three thousand worlds," has echoes in the field of physics today. The famous American physicist David Bohm (1917–1992) "believed that although the universe appears to be solid, it is, in essence, a magnificent hologram." He believed in the "whole in every part" idea, and just like a hologram, each part of physical reality contained information about the whole[1]."

Thus, we know that we may recognize the ears, hands, feet, and scalp as networks of microsystems, thereby allowing us to reach into the entire person through a small part of the body, in addition to prescribing medication or using needles.

In my many years of studying at the TCM school, I have learned numerous methods of treatment. Now and then, if I don't practice a technique in the clinic for a long time, I sometimes forget about it; one such method was auricular medicine. I've had a dubious attitude towards it even when I studied with a well-known 84-year-old professor called the "Mother of Auricular Medicine."

On the first day of a four-day intensive doctor's seminar, I was sitting in my seat listening to lectures early in the morning when I suddenly felt a sharp lower back and sciatica pain on the right side of my body. I involuntarily started tapping the trouble area with my knuckles while mumbling, "Damn, I don't want to waste time asking for an acupuncture treatment right now. What should I do?"

1. Resource from https://futurism.com/david-bohm-and-the-holographic-universe

"Use ear seeds! It won't disturb the class that way," suggested my doctor friend Flynn.

"Right! I've forgotten about that."

My friend gave me some ear seeds, helped me find the lower back and sciatica region's pressure points, and stuck the small black vegetable seeds onto my ears. I thought to myself, "What a natural way of treating pain! Even the tools are just vegetable seeds. But I'm not sure if it's going to work. Hopefully, it does."

The seminar went on, and I pressed on the tiny seeds continuously while listening to the lecture. It hurt! But constantly stimulating the pressure points is part of the ear seed treatment. No pain, no gain. I kept pressing.

Two hours passed, and when break time came, I got up and found that the sciatica pain had significantly reduced from the original pain level of seven out of ten to five! I was delighted with how effective the treatment was, so I decided to experiment out of it and left the seeds on my ear for three more days. As expected, the sciatica and lower back pain completely went away on the third day. With this successful experience of the auricular treatment, I began to use this method in my clinical practice daily.

I remember a case of helping a young woman to quit smoking. When we first started, she would smoke five packs of cigarettes a day. After a month of auricular treatment, she gradually reduced to one pack of cigarettes a day; after two months, her cigarette intake reduced to three units a day or less. Other successful cases of auricular treatment were with patients suffering from shoulder stiffness, neck pain, weight control, insomnia, high blood pressure, fever, gastritis, and more.

Many years ago, our family went on a trip during the spring season, in which we encountered a heavy traffic jam. We were stuck on the freeway for almost five hours during the Chinese New Year season. My seventy-year-old mom was eager to go to the restroom but couldn't. In a hurry, I did a hand massage on her urinary system, and after only five minutes, she told me, "I feel better now. I think I can hold it to the rest area." And she did. She held on for almost an hour to use the restroom.

Another time, I had a severe headache due to the cold from the air conditioner. My mother-in-law knows foot massage very well, so she used acupressure, pressed my big toe for ten minutes, and reduced my headache by at least ninety percent.

I have a history of cardiovascular problems such as heart failure that can become more aggravated when tired, exhausted, or catching a cold. Most of the time, I will experience shortness of breath or be unable to talk. Finally, one time I remembered to use acupressure on my palm, near the base of the thumb on the area that's in charge of the heart region. I pressed for a few minutes as a first-aid method, and soon I was able to breathe again.

Dennis Gabor, people called him "The father of Holographic."The Nobel Prize in Physics 1971.Prize motivation: "for his invention and development of the holographic method." After Gabor's Nobel Prize, it becomes easier to let people understand and apply to promote TCM Holographic therapy with many believers. Enabled us to better understand the thousand years ago TCM auricular therapy, foot reflexology, scalp needles, or acupuncture often treating disease in the upper part by managing the lower, or vise versa; treating disease in the left body managing the right, or vice versa. Hologram therapy is a fantastic gift we have inherited from ancient wisdom, and I am genuinely grateful for it.

All it takes is one small change to launch the whole body; a tiny shift can affect everything, just like the butterfly effect.

Dr. Jessie Lee

Body Part Holographic Relationships

Tongue

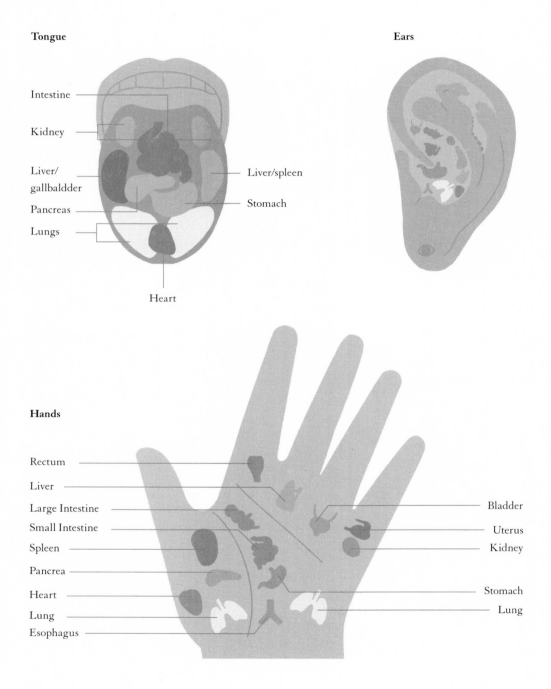

Intestine

Kidney

Liver/
gallbaldder

Pancreas

Lungs

Heart

Liver/spleen

Stomach

Ears

Hands

Rectum

Liver

Large Intestine

Small Intestine

Spleen

Pancrea

Heart

Lung

Esophagus

Bladder

Uterus

Kidney

Stomach

Lung

Feet

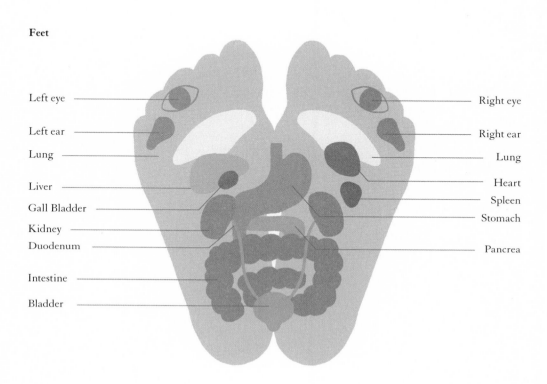

Left eye ——————— ——————— Right eye

Left ear ——————— ——————— Right ear

Lung ——————— ——————— Lung

Liver ——————— ——————— Heart

Gall Bladder ——————— ——————— Spleen

Kidney ——————— ——————— Stomach

Duodenum ——————— ——————— Pancrea

Intestine ———————

Bladder ———————

Scalp

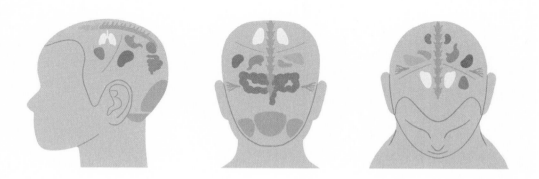

Infant Care

Caress and massage gently
to transfer healing and love.

Dr. Jessie Lee

My youngest patient was a newborn boy, only twenty-five days old. His mom used to come to see me for her health maintenance. The mom carried her baby into the clinic and explained worriedly, "He had a low fever last week and a low appetite, and he cried so much. We took him to the emergency room, and the hospital kept him for four days to do a cerebral spinal fluid examination through the L3, L4 spinal cord to make sure he didn't have meningitis. Thank goodness there was nothing especially wrong with him, so the hospital sent us home. But he has maintained a low fever and is still fussy."

Immediately upon examination, I found purple-red veins on the outside of the baby's index finger, which in TCM is a way to help to diagnose children under 2-3 years of age. Purple-red veins mean that a newborn baby has an internal heat pattern that is mildly out of balance. I taught the mom how to check for this and how to help the baby. We used an acupressure technique specific to children by quickly rubbing a finger about 300-500 times in a minute, in an upward direction, on the affected area to expel the internal heat. The baby was soon brought back to equilibrium and felt calm and balanced; he ceased crying, and his face became pink and light.

This newborn had been suffering from digestive stagnation, which caused abdominal upset with internal heat. I poked a needle quickly for one second into his leg ST.36 stomach point but didn't leave it in. (Infants and small children can benefit from quick insertions of acupuncture needles without keeping the needles on the body for a while.)

I also taught the mom how to gently stroke the infant's spinal cord, a unique soft stroke technique that uses acupressure. It's simple and easy but helps maintain a healthy immune system so that the baby won't get sick often.

After one month, the baby came again, and this time, I saw his forehead was pale green. I asked the mom, "Did you shock the baby by slamming a door? Or did you take him to a crowded place?"

"Hmm... I don't think we shocked the baby with any loud sounds at home, but, yes, I took him out to a shopping mall with friends yesterday, and then at midnight, he became inconsolable, crying a lot. "

I didn't use needles on the baby; I used an obsidian pillar to clean his energy. Amazingly, after only 2 seconds of waving the crystal around the baby, he suddenly became reticent, and his eyes opened wide. He observed us silently. After about five minutes of the obsidian cleaning process, the baby was very calm and not at all annoyed. This therapy kept him peaceful for about a month until the next time he got out of balance.

My favorite infant soft-touch rubbing method for

- Calm mood
- Upset stomach
- Colds, cough
- Vomiting , diahrrhea, or constipation
- Stunting

Precautions

- Don't do it when there is no professional guidance.
- Requires rubbing direction into a straight line, not back and forth
- Trim nails and make sure they are clean.
- Strictly follow the clockwise or counterclockwise direction of the abdomen.
- Never press on the head because the baby "fontanels" or soft spots are still developing.
- Never press hard on the abdomen because the baby's bones and organs are still fragile. It is recommended to gently press the back or limbs.

Checking Index Fingers On Babies

Color	Present	How to Balance
Bright red	External wind-cold	Expels external wind-cold
Purple-red	Heat pattern (internal heat)	300-500 times/min upward outward direction to expel the internal heat
Green-blue	Fright wind, pain pattern, or ate bad food	To calm mind and tonify
Sallow pale	Deficiency pattern	200-300 times/min inward direction
Purple-black	Depressed heat blocking the blood networks	Unblock circulation

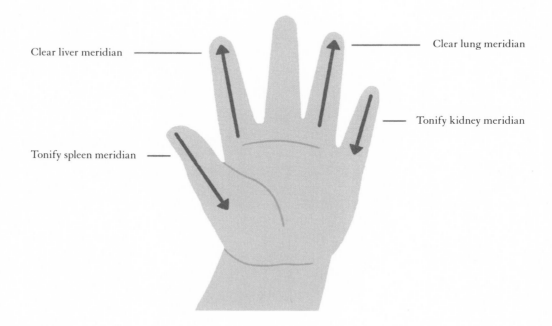

Clear liver meridian

Clear lung meridian

Tonify kidney meridian

Tonify spleen meridian

Infant Massage

Gently massage in the direction indicated, 200-300 times per minute.

Infant Constipation

On the side of the index finger, massage from the base of the finger to the tip.

Massage gently clockwise on the infant's abdomen.

Massage gently upwards from the base of the tail bone to the lower back.

Infant Fever

On the inside of the forearm, massage downwards from the base of the hand to the crook of the elbow.

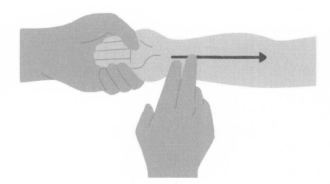

Infant Upset Stomach

General stomach issues, vomiting, diarrhea, constipation, colds, cough, stunting, or general calming.

While the infant is on its belly, gently massage upwards on the back.

Acupuncture Practitioner Journey

Why Warm

Life is a gentle, smooth, and warm energy flow.

TCM Saying

For over three years, a nurse in her mid-eighties came to see me to treat her swollen right ankle due to a past car accident. Westerners often try acupuncture for their unresolved long-term sicknesses and pains after they have tried everything else to no avail.

It was the woman's first time undergoing acupuncture, so I took some time to explain what the needles would feel like, described the energy flows, and introduced her to the concept of meridians. I needed to be gentle while inserting needles. Newcomers to acupuncture are often sensitive to needles and initially respond better to smaller, shorter, and fewer needles.

The elderly nurse responded well to her first forty-minute acupuncture session, and she left the clinic relaxed and happy. But to help her heal better and faster, I gave her some homework:

"Soak your feet with warm water for at least twenty to thirty minutes every day. And make sure the warm water depth comes up to the calf region," I instructed her.

She looked surprised and asked, "Warm water? We usually use ice! I've never heard of using warm water."

"Yes, use warm water."

"But why? We only use ice."

"May I ask you a question? Did the ice help to heal your ankle? Did the icing effect last a long time? If icing worked out, then why are you here? Why don't you give the other way a try? This icing method might not be the best for all injuries."

"Hmm...When I used ice, it made the pain go away for maybe thirty minutes, but it always came back. I will give warm water a try, but could you tell me why?"

"Is our body warm?"

"It's warm, of course."

"That's it! We all know the normal human body temperature is 36.5-37.5 °C (97.7– 99.5 °F). This warm water keeps our metabolism, digestion, and all of the circulatory systems functioning. When a river meets icy temperatures, it will slow down the flow and eventually freeze; likewise, the human body's circulation stagnates with cold."

In the West, ice is commonly used after acute muscle strains to block pain. Icing restricts blood flow to the area, which helps to numb pain and keeps initial swelling from getting out of control.

The Chinese Yellow Emperor's Classic of Internal Medicine teaches us that the human body prefers warmth to function more efficiently, particularly for the stomach and spleen; otherwise, those organs will be shocked by the cold and be unable to digest properly. Our heart and small intestine have the characteristics of "fire" and therefore need heat force to perform their tasks.

For example, the food won't be cooked thoroughly if the flame is not strong enough to cook on the stove. With a long-term cold diet, drinking ice water, our digestive systems become damaged. They can't effectively transform food into energy, causing our metabolisms to slow, delaying recovery from injuries, and contributing to chronic conditions such as obesity and fatigue.

The global climate is warming; many of our illnesses come from "wind-cold" due to the excessive use of air-conditioning, cold drinks, ice cream, and insufficient clothing that does not protect the body from the cold. Although the icy treats and air conditioning bring us temporary comforts, we still need to maintain balance to achieve a healthy life.

Even people who naturally "run hot" and have a habit of drinking icy beverages should try to move toward consuming room temperature liquids to avoid extremes that, over prolonged use, can cause the body to fall out of equilibrium and become vulnerable to illness.

Exercise Healing Life Energy Flow

Treat the body as a temple, do exercises:
QiGong, Tai-Chi, yoga, dance, and more...
Try to exercise first; don't overdo treatment.

In the busy stream of life, it's rare for me to have an afternoon break. But one day, there were no more errands, I suddenly had an afternoon all to myself, and I felt tired. Time to take a nap!

I quickly fell into a profound sleep for two hours without any dreams or interruptions. When I woke up, it was already dark, and time to make dinner. I stood up and got ready to go downstairs to cook, but I found that the entire left side of my body hurt from head to toe, almost like it had suffered a stroke. I had a terrible migraine on the left side of my head, and my left shoulder was stiff and sore, my left hip joint hurt, my left knee cap ached, and my left ankle and toes were also in stiffness pain.

"Please… just give me a break," I thought, frustrated. "What's wrong with me? Why can't I even take a little nap!?"

I was upset, but I still dragged my body downstairs and made dinner grudgingly despite the pains and aches. All the while, I was thinking, should I use needles? Take herbs? What formula of herbs should I take?

After forty minutes, I placed dinner on the table and called the children to eat. I went back upstairs without eating, still feeling upset and wondering how to fix myself. I was sick of everything! I'd always used needles and herbs in the past; it was time to try something else.

An idea suddenly popped into my head: why not practice Tai-Chi or QiGong Ba Duan Jin? It is a form of exercise taught by my first TCM teacher, Dr. Song, in Mexico. I practiced it for a few months but discontinued it because, at that time, I had Qi deficiency and became dizzy every time I practiced.

Thanks to the convenience of YouTube, I found a few videos teaching Ba Duan Jin. I carefully watched a fifteen-minute demonstration video, trying to remember what the teacher taught me, and began to practice. At first, my body was stiff, and the pain on the left side worsened. But as I slowly moved and took careful breaths, my movement became smoother and less strained, the soreness and pain seemed to decrease.

I continued, focusing harder. After about fifteen minutes of exercising, I determined that the pain had decreased by at least forty percent, so I kept at it again and again. After thirty minutes, the pain and stiffness were gone entirely, and my body was warm from all the blood flowing smoothly through my veins.

I was full of gratitude. Feeling happy, light, and healthy, I headed downstairs to have dinner. The children saw me and said, "You fixed yourself! You look so much happier! Have you done acupuncture? Are you feeling better now? "

I told them, "Look, the acupuncture theory always says, "where there is a blockage, there will be pain. With body aches, there must be a stagnation." This time I didn't use any needles or herbs. I just practiced Qigong Ba Duan Jin and used body energy flow to remove my meridians' blockage. That's why exercise is so important! I am impressed now by my experience."

I am an active person, and grew up practicing various sports: swimming, track, volleyball, hiking, and gym class. But when getting older, I easily got injuries on my joints during my menopause, so I have to start with other slow and smoother exercises like Tai-Chi, Yoga, or QiGong Ba Duan Jin. Finally, I stick with Ba Duan Jin because it's only eight steps easier to remember with a good energy flow result.

Treat the body as a temple, respect the body, exercise, practice Qigong, Tai-Chi, yoga or dance, and more. Make the body healthy and love everything the body gives us. Through the body's five senses, our spirit can experience the beautiful world and create binary opposition Yin and Yang space. We should respect this incredible, fantastic system - the body.

Every living thing has Qi - the life energy flow in our body. Only I can decide if I want to use it to restore my health or not. I am the only one responsible.

It's time to move and exercise!

Eight Section Qigong Exercise - Ba Duan Jin

第一段
雙手托天理三焦
Prop up the sky with two hands to improve Tri-Jiao.

第二段
左右開弓似射鵰
Draw back arms on both sides as if shooting a bow.

第五段
五勞七傷往後瞧
Look back to treat five strains and impairments.

第六段
雙手攀足護腎腰
Bend to touch the toes to reinforce the kidneys.

第三段
調理脾胃舉單手
Raise a single arm to regulate the spleen and stomach.

第四段
搖頭擺尾去心火
Shake the head and wag the tail to expel heart fire.

第七段
轉拳怒目增力氣
Clench one's fist and glare to increase strength.

第八段
背後起點舊病消
Rise and fall on tiptoes seven times to treat all diseases.

Sleep Healing
& Twelve
Circadian Cycle

Rise with the sun, rest with the sunset.

Chinese Proverb

One day, my daughter sent a brief message from Portland. She asked, "Mum, I've been falling asleep within the first fifteen minutes of reading a book. What's going on?"

I replied, "First, it means that your body is telling you that you need to sleep more and to get enough rest to replenish your energy. Have you been busy lately or stay late at night? Second, during every seasonal transition, the body needs to adjust to the pace of the climate. It is particularly tiring because the body uses extra energy to adjust to and keep up with the solar terms' rhythms. If we catch any pathological illnesses from external factors, the body needs more energy to recover. That's why you feel extra tired."

Now, sleep is a great topic to touch on. From my personal experience, ever since I became a mother, I've had a sleep deficit for many years. Taking care of my children on top of working is like a candle with both ends on fire. During the prime of my life, raising children and working used most of my energy. It drained me faster than I could recharge, and my body became weak; headaches, stomach pains, and skin allergies constantly plagued me. My sisters often called me "Lin Dai Yu 林黛玉," a famous novel about an elegant lady who got sick daily. It occurred when I was only twenty-five to thirty-five years old.

And then, when I was working in Mexico City, the high-stress work schedule continued to aggravate the burden on my body. I worked six days a week, and on Sundays, I would study TCM at the university. There was no rest during the entire week, except for national and seasonal holidays. When I slept, I felt as if I hadn't slept for hundreds of years. Life was a high-speed sprint in every aspect for many years. My body often shuts down in the dusk, feeling tired. My TCM professor Dr. Song called me "Sunflower" and warned me that long-term physical overdraft harms one's health. I knew it by my brain, but I kept working and studying without resting. Gastritis, stomach ulcer, headaches, allergies, many chronic illnesses, and even "Barrett's Esophagus," a serious per-cancer illness, came to me. This happened while I was age thirty-six to forty-two.

Drawing lessons from bitter experience, I finally decided to slow down the pace. The student life of studying for master's and doctorate degrees in the States became simple, disciplined, and straightforward. But there would still be very sleepy and tired days. When that happened, I would let go of everything and take a nap, allow myself to get some good rest.

According to TCM, circadian activity rhythms shift every two hours for each meridian; midday 11:00 to 13:00 is when the Heart system rebuilds its energies. It's good to take a main meal of the day and then take a brief rest for ten to twenty minutes, making the whole afternoon vivid and not affecting the night's sleep. Whenever I did these naps, it usually turned into a deep, good quality sleep. This rest helps me regain energy and clear my mind; I feel refreshed and healthy, and the effects last for days.

Many patients have asked, "If I stay up late at night, but I wake up later the next day, it's a total of eight hours. Does it count?"

"No, because according to the TCM biological clock, 23:00 to 3:00 midnight is the time for the Gallbladder and Liver's to repair and detox. We don't want to suppress it when it's working for itself. We need to be in the deep sleep state, and detox the Liver and blood system." We can't owe sleep debts, otherwise, we are going to pay back with health issues.

When my menopause started, at the age of fifty, I could no longer stay up late. If I don't sleep well or get enough sleep, I feel frustrated easily. Gradually, I have adjusted my bedtime to 10:00 PM. As soon as I am sleepy, I go to bed and fall asleep quickly. The next day I wake up when the sunrises, full of energy and recharged. But if I wake up tired and my body feels heavy and exhausted, then I know that I've been "invaded by external factors."

About menopause, also has been mentioned the pattern in the human's biological rhythm. In the medical book Yellow Emperor's Classic of Internal Medicine, Huangdi Neijing 黃帝內經 indicate that women's growth pattern are multiples of seven, men are multiples of eight.

For women, at the age of fourteen (2X7), her menstruation begins to appear. By the age of twenty-one (3X7), her wisdom teeth have grown up. By the age of twenty-eight (4X7), her body is in its strongest stage. By the age of thirty-five (5X7), her physique begins to decline gradually. By the age of forty-two (6X7), her face becomes wane, and her hair begins to turn white. By the age of forty-nine (7X7), her physique turns old and feeble, and by then, the menopause stage starts.

For men, at the age of sixteen (2X8), he is filled with vital energy and can let out sperm. By the age of twenty-four (3X8), his kidney energy is well developed to reach an adult's state. By the age of thirty-two (4X8), his whole body has grown to its best condition and strength. By the age of forty (5X8), his kidney energy turns gradually from prosperous to decline. As a result, his hairs begin to fall, and teeth start to weaken. At the age of forty-eight (6X8), his complexion withers and his hair becomes white. After the age of fifty-six (7X8), his liver energy declines; as the liver determines the tendons' condition, they will become rigid and loose their nimbleness. After the age of sixty-four (8X8), his tendons and bones weakness, his essence and vital energy decline, his teeth fall off, and every part of his body becomes decrepit. Men's menopause stage starts.

Talking about sleep, I had a very typical clinical case of using a sleep healing method to heal a severe case of recurring hives and eczema. A patient came with twenty years of chronic eczema. The problem of severe eczema started when he was a child. He had tried many doctors and therapists, dermatology, immunology, internal medicine, nutrition, spinal etiology, Chinese medicine, and acupuncture in the previous years. All provided minor improvements, but it always came back with a vengeance. I paid particular attention to balancing his cervical spine system, helping with the autonomic nerve systems, endocrine system, and stabilizing his immunity. I gradually recognized that the problem came from his habits and everyday lifestyle: he liked to stay up late, which made him lack energy; he ate seafood, which would have triggered allergies.

After a few months of hard work to stabilize his skin condition, he would think that he has been cured and returned to his old habits. He would start eating his favorite kinds of seafood, and within a couple of hours, his skin would again begin to fester and the allergic reaction would be more severe each time.

Then came the final incident. During a vacation to visit home, the patient ate seafood as usual. It detonated his system, and severe eczema appeared all over his skin, even oozing pus from the red, swollen patches. He visited with doctors again, but could not effectively relieve the symptoms. He ultimately gave up all treatments and flew back to California. He was jet-lagged and exhausted, so he slept a lot. He slept for more than twelve hours a day and ate mainly plain rice congee, a simple food. After just sleeping and eating plain rice porridge for a month and a half, his skin problems slowly but miraculously began to heal.

During the time he spent sleeping, his parasympathetic nerves calmed down. Combined with the gentle diet, his body healed itself. After this painstaking healing process, he got to know his body more and more; first, he realized he needed enough good quality sleep; and second, he had to pay attention to what he eats, taking special care to avoid the foods that could trigger his allergies for a while until the body stably healed. Now, it's been more than one year, and his skin remains well.

Being mindful and recognizing patterns in our sleep quality and diet concerning how the body reacts is very important and helps build harmonizing habits.

Five self-checking tips to maintain body health

- Sleep well.
- Poop well. (After defecation, observe the stool before flushing.)
- Eat well.
- Drink good quality water.
- Tongue looks well. (Observe when brushing teeth.)

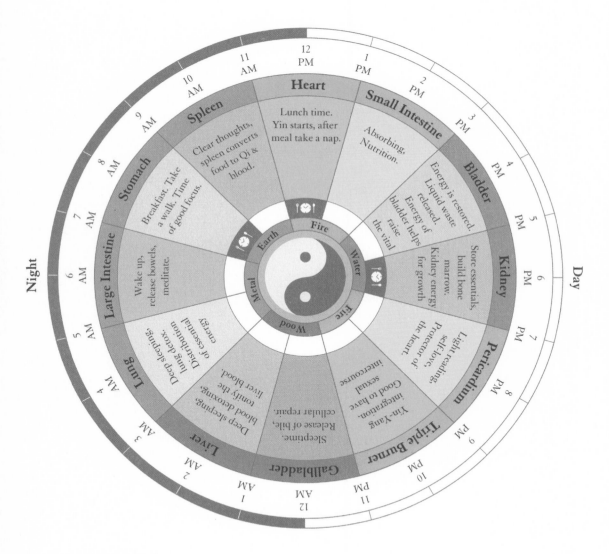

Time Zone: GMT+8

16/8
Intermittent Fasting

I never cease to learn new healing methods.
I know birth, aging, sickness, and death
still run their course, but by understanding
the universal laws of nature and myself,
I can live in harmony, and carry the hope of
a more harmonious life.

Dr. Jessie Lee

The number of "2/168" reminds me that a week is 168 hours; I receive an acupuncture treatment two hours a week, I am responsible for the other 168 hours with myself since I am with my body all the time. Now, another number I experienced, "16/8" is about intermittent fasting.

Due to my chronic cholecystitis, with a three year history of recurrent severe right hypochondrial pain after eating fatty or acidic foods, I have to be aware of what I eat. Still, I often accidentally eat the wrong food. Without being aware I would mistakenly eat certain foods and suffer stomach bloating, right swollen costal pain, headache, vomiting, right shoulder pain, fatigue, and more. It mainly happens during the 11PM to 3AM time frame – the Gallbladder and Liver system circadian cycle period. I used to fix myself with acupuncture or guasha or hit my back against the wall to promote energy flow during the midnight. If all those methods don't relieve the pain though, I wake up my partner to help me with emergency treatment.

I did the so-called "gall-bladder flushing" or "liver cleansing" regimen; this regime consisted of a free intake of apples and vegetable juice but no food for a few days, followed by the consumption of olive oil and lemon juice over several hours. This activity resulted in the passage of multiple semisolid green or dark brown "things" per rectum in the early hours of the following day. But this regimen did not help me, and I experienced lots of abdominal pain with vomiting. That experience let me understand that everyone is unique. What is good for others is not really good for me. Personalized medicine is needed. And many years later, I finally learned of a cutting-edge natural medicine's "Bioenergetic Sensitivity Test" method that distinguishes six types of people and helped me know myself more and more. I'm a type less resistant and more sensitive to the relay of energy. I often feel discomfort or suffer conspicuous side effects when I take the dosage prescribed by my physician. That's why I choose natural healing and energy healing methods for my life. By contrast, for those who are more resistant and less sensitive to energy, the dosage and the healing speed should vary with the sensitivity of the person.

Therefore, I try other methods: 16/8 intermittent fasting (dinner before 17:00 and take breakfast next day at 9:00) three weeks a year; 16 hours with only taking water, eight hours eating quality meals, veggies, and fruits. It could be adjusted by everyone's body condition, like 15/9 (dinner before 17:00 and take breakfast next day at 8:00) or 14/10 (dinner before 18:00 and take breakfast next day at 8:00).

And I found this did help me a lot; better digestion and improved sleep quality (such as not waking up from 11:00 pm to 5:30 am); the good sleep helped my brain with clarity, productivity, and emotion in the harmonic state. It has been a while since I became a mother; I didn't sleep well for the longest time. Usually, I slept light and was easy woken up by even the tiniest sound. I was too alert, and too nervous to take care of children. The sympathetic nerve system was overactive.

During the intermittent fasting period, my gallbladder and liver system gets complete rest and rebuild their strength to function. The important circadian period of the gallbladder and liver is 23:00 to 3:00. With the last meal at 18:00, we have enough time to digest and don't burden our gallbladder and liver to working hard at midnight and disturb our sleep. Some patients even mentioned that this intermittent fasting helped them lose weight.

According to TCM, the liver system manages: purifies the bacteria, virus, restores blood, manages eyes, tendons, hair, nails, and maintains the body's energy flow system. Therefore, dysmenorrhea, sciatica, shoulder pain, trigger finger, tendon issues, vision issues, skin allergies… they're all related to liver and gallbladder function.

Diet &
Body Types

As I am aging and have gone through
a cycle of several decades; I have
experienced different diet programs.

By knowing which body type we fit into
based on Yin & Yang, and the foods to
balance it — this is the best diet balancing
guideline.

I figured out my body constitution type
was a mix of wind and fire elements.
What's yours?

Dr. Jessie Lee

I suffered from frequent severe skin allergies for up to nine years from when I was sixteen. When I was in Guatemala, I loved to eat ceviche twice a week, and I did that for almost four months. One day, two hours after I had eaten ceviche, hundreds of patches of extremely itchy rashes appeared suddenly on both of my arms. The itching caused me to stay up all night, scratching, unable to fall asleep. It took about ten days to recover gradually. From then on, I got an allergic reaction whenever I touched seafood. I soon also began having allergic reactions to beef, pork, and chicken.

Because of these incidents and my love for animals, I decided to become a vegetarian when I was twenty-five. My skin allergies finally stopped for years. After twenty-three years of being a vegetarian, my body went to the opposite extreme cold state, bringing the allergy issue back. After learning TCM and gaining knowledge about how the body keeps changing, I need to be aware of the changes. Listen to my body, adjust what I eat. I began eating small portions of meat and fish while keeping my diet ninety-five percent vegetarian, adding warm property foods, and taking sunbaths to balance my cold with good sleep. I am feeling healthy and vigorous again until the present.

I remember the first formal diet training class I attended when I was twenty-eight years old. After my father's third stroke, we were saddened that my sisters and I lacked the Chinese medicine skill set to help our father, but it also led us to take immediate action to go back to school to learn TCM and natural therapy. Once I read a book about the story of an American lady who has successfully recovered from a stroke by following an organic diet program. I did a lot of research, and two weeks after I read the book, I flew to California from Guatemala with my three-year-old daughter to participate in a three-week residential self-improvement program in San Diego. We would learn about nutritional, physical, mental, emotional, and spiritual harmony, which is also in a diet program. The institute was nestled on a four-acre hilltop among stately trees, with a serene atmosphere prevailing on campus. I learned wheat grass planting, sprouting, enema skills, and how to apply them to our daily life to detoxify our bodies.

I loved the part of sauerkraut making, organic gardening, and food preparation class. There was a fat white cat who came to visit our townhouse during our stay in San Diego. My little daughter played quietly with the cat for the entire day, she never once complained to me that she had no friends or was bored, thanks to that cat's company.

I lost sixteen pounds after that three-week diet program even though I was a relatively healthy person with no severe illness. Still, I followed the diet plan, participated in all courses, and got my completion certificate. I needed to learn by experience, and then I would know how to help my father. In the end, although he didn't recover the abilities to do his daily tasks, the organic diet cleansed his body. His usual dark and rough face turned baby soft and light. The diet also helped control my father's high blood pressure.

When I got my certificate and left the institute, I drove back to greater LA to meet with a friend and share about that three-week experience. In the parking lot, I walked past an elderly bearded American man. We looked at each other, and as I nodded my head to greet him, a thought suddenly popped into my head, "Is he the author of the Iridology book? Who can diagnose by examining the iris of the eye? Funny, where did that thought come from? I have never read that book or even seen the author's picture. Of course, I don't know him." I laughed to myself.

But, when I walked into the restaurant with my daughter, the waiter said, "You are so lucky today."

"Why?" I asked.

"Because a great master is here today in this restaurant."

"Oh, Really? Who is it?"

"The author who can diagnose illnesses through looking at the eyeball."

"Wow! That's interesting. Can you show me where this master is now?"

The waitress pointed, and to my surprise, it was the same man I met in the parking lot. But how did I know he was the author of the book?

It looked like the cleansing diet enhanced my intuition. I was twenty-eight years old. I kept the diet for another five years after I left San Diego, although my two TCM doctor sisters have always warned me: "Jessie, according to TCM, you'd better have a more diverse diet and cook warm foods to keep a balance. It's too cold if you only eat raw vegetables"

I told them, "I am fine, don't worry, I feel great! Energized and alert."I didn't realize a health crisis was approaching. At the age of thirty, I had my second child naturally inclined to cold body constitution, and he was born to be a vegetarian, different from his other two siblings. This experience shows me how the physique of a pregnant mother affects the fetus directly. After his birth, due to a lack of warm energy in my body to promote blood function for the Heart system, I experienced severe depression for a second time and fatigue for quite a while.

From my experience, I learned that an extreme diet for an extended period could bring our body to another outer side and then out of balance. Like bipolar mental disorder, two extremes contrary emotions. Short-term diet programs are okay, but adjust according to the body's needs is important to stay balanced.

When I was treating Barrett's Esophagus at age forty, I couldn't have lemon juice, apples, chilies, and coffee for two and a half years! Those are my favorite foods; I have always loved these foods very much since childhood, but during my illness they made me nauseous and caused stomachaches, so I had to quit them for years until my body healed itself. Now I can enjoy my favorite foods and drinks once more. But still, I have to be aware, and not indulge in excess.

Besides acupuncture, I always talk about lifestyles with my patients, eating habits, and stress states. One day a familiar patient came to me with irritation - red eyes and a dry throat. In the beginning, I couldn't figure out why, but during our pre-acupuncture chat, the patient told me happily, "I went to visit families in my hometown. They have a ranch with a lot of sheep, so they cooked lamb for me every day. I ate lamb for the entire week. It was delicious."

"Bingo, that's it! Now I know what caused your body's inner heat excess. Lamb's properties are very hot. Many Asians know that, so we only eat it during the winter or feed people who are weak and cold. But only eat in small quantities. Some people get nose bleeds after eating lamb."

Then I put some needles on the points that clear fire to cool down her body and recommended a week of herbal supplements with cold properties to cleanse the excess heat body. The following week the patient came back with a better-balanced state, feeling happier and refreshed.

A sixty-year-old lady's hemorrhoids had been going on for thirty years without knowing why; after a period of treatment and discussion, finally, we found every time she eats spicy, fatty foods or when stressed, her hemorrhoids return. Ever since she started regular weekly acupuncture, her body condition has maintained stable for a year. Then, she stopped coming for three months due to the Covid-19 "shelter in place" order. When the city reopened, she came back immediately and said, "Dr. Lee, I have to come back for regular acupuncture sessions because I have been feeling tired and stressed, I have insomnia, and my hemorrhoids are back."

During the treatment session, I found that her skin bruised easily, and her bleeding from small wounds would take much longer than usual to stop, both of which didn't happen before. I was baffled. As usual, I asked many questions about food, drinks, and activities, but there were no clues.

The third week, her husband came along, and he asked me, "Dr. Lee, nowadays we eat turmeric every day with rice. Is that okay?"

"Turmeric? How long have you been taking that?" I asked.

"Since the city was locked down, we heard from a friend that turmeric is good for health, and we don't want to get COVID, so it has been about four months."

I went to my patient and told her, "I think I've found the cause of your problems. You'd better stop taking turmeric to see if the symptoms go away. Because turmeric has hot properties and is not suitable for you, but it is okay for your husband."

Her symptoms recovered after she stopped taking turmeric for about three weeks, and her body came back to a balanced and comfortable state.

It's the Yin-Yang cold and hot theory, but there are more details according to TCM theory. Everything is constantly changing: everything has its Yin, Yang, cold and hot; five elements with five physical body constitutions, five colors of food, five types of flavors, and more.

In TCM, we diagnose problems, and the resulting treatment plan will either emphasize to tonify a weak element or sedate an excessive part to restore homeostasis state. Usually, we use the food's flavor test properties to sedate and use its color properties to tonify.

Here, I will briefly explain five body types with five flavors and five colors of food interaction. We all have a few other elements mixed with our constitution. However, we still can find a dominant element by classifying the general physical appearance, personality characteristics, and susceptible diseases of the people living in different regions and summarizing five different physiques, the earliest attempts at diagnoses of Taoist doctors' systematic classification of patients.

Another important systematic classification of patients is the TCM cosmic part: "Wu Yun Liu Qi 五運六氣 Five Movements & Six Energies- 5Y6Q". We play a role in understanding a person's natural-born constitution by birth date. We're born with the package and have our gifts and challenges related to it, and that is what we said to be our Five Element Constitution type. I am going to explain more in the next chapter.

With all these different classifications, it's the pathway I've gone through to know about myself, and it gives me relief to know why I am the way I am, so I'm passing this self-understanding skill to my patients. Many have told me that it comes as a relief to them too. We are what we eat; food is medicine, everybody is unique, and we should learn how to harmonize. We must be aware of the properties of the foods we eat.

Recommended foods for Wind-Fire types like myself include bitter and sour foods because the taste of bitterness belongs to fire, and sour belongs to the wind. Eat grains, vegetables, dark leafy greens, seeds, and beans. These foods tend to keep the fire at bay, with no overabundance. Foods to avoid include meats, salt, chocolate, hot spices, and stimulants. I would guard against becoming too susceptible like the blowing wind, slowing down my fast reactions, holding my excessive compassion and emotions, respecting others' life missions, and leaving space for others, plus increased quality of alone time.

But always keep in mind that self-cultivation with wisdom helps to modify the Five Types of body constitution and personality. It's not so absolute that it couldn't change.

Here is a simple chart to help you have some ideas; I've kept them brief, but there's much more to say. I encourage you to study more as there's plenty of useful information on the Internet, or you can consult with your TCM doctor.

We classified food into five properties as cold, cool, neutral, warm, and hot.

Relationship of Five Organs & Emotions

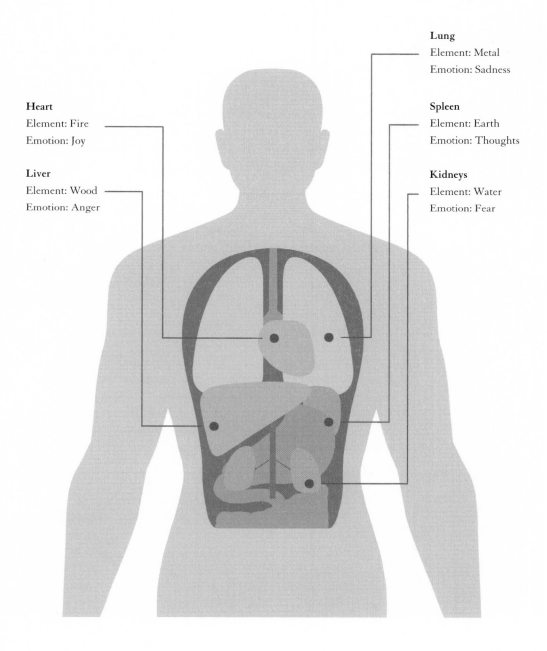

Heart
Element: Fire
Emotion: Joy

Liver
Element: Wood
Emotion: Anger

Lung
Element: Metal
Emotion: Sadness

Spleen
Element: Earth
Emotion: Thoughts

Kidneys
Element: Water
Emotion: Fear

Five Elements	Five Body Types & Characters
Wood	Spring and wind related. Tends to be slender or tiny like a tree, and grows up steadfast. Physical qualities often include a long face, body & fingers. Determined, active, fast-thinking, competitive, adventurous. Novel, moves like the wind. The liver, gallbladder, tendons, ligaments and sinews are ruled by the wood element. Seeks out challenges and does well under pressure, but can become driven, stressed, irritable & impatient when out of balance. Tends to overwork.
Fire	Summer and heat related. Robust with warm palms and feet. May have ruddy complexions and prominent cheekbones. They sometimes have red hair and freckles, a red tongue and dry stool. Tends to sweat easily, and likes cold drinks. Related to the circulatory, glandular & immune systems. This includes the heart, small intestine and lymphatic system. Personality is like summer: when balanced, is joyful, fun & exciting. Easily connect with others and has creative thoughts.
Earth	Late summer, related to dampness. Earth people often have square faces & jaws, large mouths, a short stature, short fingers and neck. The body is pear shaped with rounded buttocks. Some may show a pale greasy face. Easily gets diarrhea when the Earth element is weak, since it rules the digestive & structural systems including the stomach, spleen and muscles. Their character may be calm, grounded, slow, and practical. Their thoughtful nature usually leads them into a caring or negotiating profession.
Metal	Fall, related to dryness. This type often has strong muscular bodies, a defined oval face, widely set cheekbones, square shoulders, thin lips &eyelids, and dry skin. Tends to be thirsty and easily constipated. Farsighted, steady, a leader; self-disciplined, organized, good at solving problems. The metal element rules the intestinal, respiratory and skin systems, and assists with the immune system. Good professions for this type include lawyers, teachers, or counselors.
Water	Winter, and cold-related.This type tends to have a large round face, big ears, chubby bottom-heavy bodies, dark hair, and soft eyes. Water types are good at going with the flow, persevering and getting things done with strong will, have a lot of determination and are fearless, but sometimes schemes and does not speak up. The water element rules the kidneys, bones, bladder, nerves and teeth. Can sometimes feel withdrawn and anxious when out of balance.

Associated Health Issues	How To Balance	Five Color Foods
PMS, irregular menstrual cycle, high blood pressure, tight muscles, headaches. Easily gets allergies. Being wound up sometimes causes cravings for chocolate, alcohol, ice cream or other unhealthy ways to relieve stress. Can easily develop addictive habits & overindulge.	Take herbs to support the liver and female hormones. Do regular slow exercises such as yoga and Tai Chi, with plenty of rest. Avoid sugar and hot, spicy foods. Learn to be flexible. Take time to play. Avoid alcohol. Be careful with sour foods.	Green foods are good for wood types. Consume foods like asparagus, green veggies, kiwi, spinach, green apples, and cruciferous vegetables..
Prone to circulatory problems, cardiovascular disease, palpitations, and sudden death. Also prone to anxiety and insomnia. May suffer skin conditions such as acne and rashes.	Include bitter foods in the diet. Leafy greens, vegetables, grains, beans & seeds. Practice meditation to calm the mind, and avoid competitive activities. Take time to be alone. Eat foods with cool properties such as cucumbers & pears. Avoid spicy, grilled and fried foods.	Red foods are good for fire types. Eat foods like cherries, tomatoes, beets, red apples, strawberries, radishes and pomegranates.
Vulnerable to digestive issues, constipation, loose stools, hemorrhoids, and fatigue. May become overweight, develop cravings for carbohydrates and sweets, and suffer bloating, gas and diarrhea.	Take care of the Spleen system. Avoid damp areas. Consistently be exercise. Avoid sweets & fatty food. Consume root veggies, leafy greens, light proteins like legumes and fish. Avoid sour food, dairy, highly processed foods, refined carbohydrates and iced drinks	Yellow foods are good for earth types. Eat foods like potatoes, corn, pumpkins, yellow peppers, pineapples, and yellow kiwi.
Prone to illnesses of the respiratory system such as asthma and lung illnesses like coughs and bronchitis. Can develop allergies & skin rashes. Prone to grief. This type is also prone to constipation.	Practice regular aerobic exercises that makes the lungs stronger. Focus on breathing techniques. Eat foods high in minerals such as leafy greens. Foods that are naturally pungent are best for this body type. Avoid eating red meats, bitter foods, and dairy.	White foods are good for metal types. Eat foods like pears, cauliflower, turnips, tofu, potatoes, mushrooms, and garbanzo beans.
May be prone to urinary tract infections and edema. Can get sore joints and back problems. Prone to water metabolism issues, infertility, low libido, hearing issues, arthritic conditions, cold extremities, and menopausal symptoms. Dark rings appear under the eyes.	Eat herbs to support the kidneys and bladder. Practice exercises like Pilates and swimming. Consume blue, purple & black foods, seaweed and seafood. Drink plenty of pure water. Avoid stimulating foods like sugar, alcohol, & caffeine. Also avoid cold, raw foods.	Black foods are good for water types. Eat foods like black beans, black sesame seeds, black raspberries, black tea, black garlic, and black ear fungus.

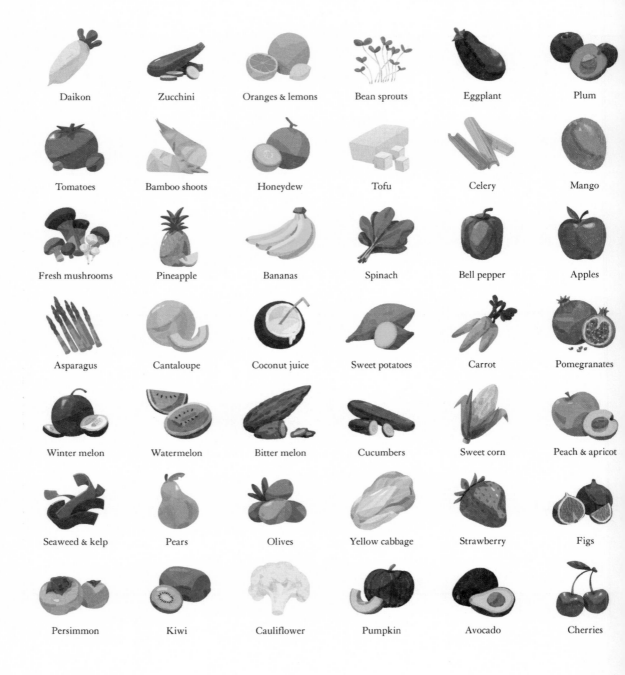

Daikon	Zucchini	Oranges & lemons	Bean sprouts	Eggplant	Plum
Tomatoes	Bamboo shoots	Honeydew	Tofu	Celery	Mango
Fresh mushrooms	Pineapple	Bananas	Spinach	Bell pepper	Apples
Asparagus	Cantaloupe	Coconut juice	Sweet potatoes	Carrot	Pomegranates
Winter melon	Watermelon	Bitter melon	Cucumbers	Sweet corn	Peach & apricot
Seaweed & kelp	Pears	Olives	Yellow cabbage	Strawberry	Figs
Persimmon	Kiwi	Cauliflower	Pumpkin	Avocado	Cherries

Cold   Cool

Dates & raisins

All kinds of beans

Potatoes

Glutinous rice

Chives

Wasabi

Lychee

Sunflower seeds

Taro

Black rice

Pistachios

Dried ginger

Milk

Pickled greens

Peanuts

Garlic

Wheat

Cumin

Mustard leaves

White cabbage

Pumpkin seeds

Basil

Scallions

Cinnamon

Bok choy

String beans & peas

Chestnuts

Fresh ginger

Star anise

Curry powder

All kinds of eggs

Cooked lotus root

Nuts

Cilantro

Pepper

Sichuan pepper

Oats

Broccoli

Dried mushrooms

Onion

Fennel

Chili

Neutral

Warm

Hot

Energy Healing Journey

Seeing Things From The Top Down

To see a world in a grain of sand, and a heaven in a wildflower. Hold infinity in the palm of your hand, and eternity in an hour.

William Blake

I always tell my patients about the concept of macro and micro universe. There is a great cosmic wheel and smaller wheels: there is a huge universe extending beyond the body, and if we look at the body, there are an infinite number of little universes inside. When the body is broken down to its core, to its smallest molecule of energy, the universe is full of powers, which means every molecule of the universe resides within the human body, considering our cells. There are roughly seven and a half billion people on our planet, and inside each one of us, there are about thirty trillion cells. The cells within the body must be a synergy of energy and blood, harmonized together.

The internal organ theories of TCM have their representative colors. The liver and gallbladder represents green; the heart and small intestine represents red; the spleen and stomach y represents yellow; the lungs and large intestine represents white; and the kidneys and bladder represents black. Each organ and cell performs its duties, and all live harmoniously together in the little universe that is our body. "I" am the cells' master, king, and savior. The state of my emotions, spirit, physical energy, and the food I eat all directly affect my cells' living environment. Therefore, whether my inner divinity is compassionate and joyful is of great importance to the little cells living inside me.

Humans are just one of the millions of species and billions of manifestations of the forces that bring together and take apart atoms through time. Seeing things from the top down is the best way to understand ourselves and the laws of the universe. That's not to say that it's not worth having a bottom-up perspective. In fact, to understand the world accurately, we need both.

By taking both the bottom-up and top-down perspectives and looking at each case, we can form bigger views, creating a panoramic picture. For example, when I started going through menopause, the left side of my neck began hurting and lasted for nearly two and a half years.

In some sense, man is a microcosm of
the universe; therefore what man is,
is a clue to the universe.
We are enfolded in the universe.

David Bohm

I treated myself with acupuncture, focusing on the cervical spinal dislocations and muscle tightness in that region. But the results were unstable, and the pain came and went often. Meanwhile, there was also a nagging dull ache in my right ankle. It wasn't until my classmates, Dr. Zhao and Dr. Wu, helped me see a bigger scale of the whole body system: I realized that my liver/gallbladder meridians were out of balance and that the problem was originating from my stressful life, emotional swings, and the weak part of my stomach system. Those things had been causing my right ankle and left neck pain for so long. Therefore, my doctor friends focused on treating the liver gallbladder digestion system and loosening my abdominal muscles' tightness, fascia layers that were pulling on my neck muscles. Meanwhile, I practiced meditation, clearing Ho'oponopono meditation to manage my emotional stress, and finally, after fourteen sessions of treatment over three months, I healed my chronic neck pain.

Until we took the macro view of my body, I had only focused on treating the area around my neck; I didn't realize that I had been straining my abdominal region, using those muscles to compensate for the work my neck muscles couldn't perform.

By looking at this nature of a situation from the top down, we can see that many of what we call "catching a cold" is just an individual body's process of adapting to the movement, including the weather and the Universe.

I always like to tell my patients that this process is like upgrading our bodies' operating systems. Yet most people are like tiny ants, focusing only on themselves and their anthills, which are like our cities, and they lose sight of the bigger picture. By exploring the self's mysteries in each manifestation of the Universe's wheel, we can understand and attain these high truths. We judge the good and the bad of things according to how we perceive them, often ignoring or forgetting to consider the bigger picture. Nature optimizes the whole, not the individual; we benefit from nature's perspective in keeping ourselves stable and balanced, as nature is much wiser than we are. Mother Nature doesn't need humans, but humans need Mother Nature.

When I am with critically ill patients or in-hospice patients, I spend more time talking about the preparations for facing death. We are all in the same boat, and it's good to help each other be brave and stay calm in faith. Once we've reached an understanding, I can usually successfully ease some of their suffering with acupuncture treatments and help them remain calm until the last minutes of their life journey.

Growing up in Latin American countries, I learned about death's cultural belief as "transformation." Despite having lost their loved ones, those who hold this belief feel plenty of peace and joy along with sadness and sorrow; they face death with a positive and colorful attitude. In contrast, other people only see pain and injustice in the end and view it as a permanent loss.

Remember that energy can't be destroyed- it can only be reconfigured. So, the same stuff is continuously falling apart and coalescing in different forms. Everything from the smallest subatomic particle to the entire galaxy is evolving. While everything apparently dies or disappears in time, the truth is that it all just gets reconfigured in evolving forms. The force behind that is evolution.

P.142, Principles by Ray Dalio

Wind Invasion

Avoid a wind as you would an arrow, avoid pretty girls as you would an enemy.

Dynasty Yuen Daoist Master Chiu Chuji (1148-1227)

In the context of this saying, "pretty girls" here refers to excessive sex, or being wanton and licentious.

One day in mid-February, a well-known patient rushed in and asked for emergency treatment. The chief complaint was as follows: middle back pain for a day; the left side was especially painful, with pain surrounding the costal rib region, making it difficult to move or breathe deeply.

When I checked the patient's pulse, I immediately could feel the lung region felt superficial, and the liver area had high tension. Her tongue showed a thick white coating, and her palms were white and greenish. Then I continued to palpate her spine system and immediately found a slight dislocation of the thoracic spine five to seven, and the muscles were tight.

She asked me worriedly, "Why is this happening? Is there a big problem?"

I said, "It's cold. You got invaded by the wind cold."

She said doubtfully, "I don't think I have a cold because there are no symptoms of a cold! I have no headaches, no nasal congestion, no sore throat."

I explained, "We Chinese doctors consider certain external factors to be invasive, and these include: wind, cold, fire, heat, dryness, dampness, bad food, and emotional stress."

I asked her, "Can you remember if you were exposed to the cold wind yesterday? Or have you become wet in the rain? Because two days ago the weather was freezing and it rained hard, and it brought beautiful snow to our local mountains."

She thought a minute and said, "No! I haven't been paying attention to the weather these days, and I didn't catch a cold."

I stopped the discussion and immediately started treatment. We continued our conversation about trivial life stories involving the family, children, and diet during New Year's Day during the treatment.

Suddenly she remembered something and said, "You know what, Dr. Lee? I recently fell in love with planting vegetables and spices in my yard. I spent a long time doing my gardening the day before yesterday. My husband was telling me to go inside the house because the wind was blowing…"

I said, "That's it! Your pulse and tongue showed me your symptoms of illness caused by the wind and cold."

Note
Exterior factors in TCM terminology includes:
wind, cold, fire, heat, dryness, dampness, bad food, emotional stress, and toxins.

"But I didn't feel the wind. I covered myself with a scarf and wore a hat and a big coat. And the sun was so shiny and beautiful. I didn't feel cold," she insisted.

"You didn't feel cold, but your body was being attack by the wind," I said. I continued to explain, "This usually isn't a problem for young people who are generally strong, but I know your body condition as my patient. You are in the unstable menopausal period, and your body is fragile and cannot stand the wind, not to mention squatting in the yard for many hours. Once the wind exterior energy factors enter the human body through the skin and the 'wind pool' point in the neck, it begins to run through the twelve meridians in sequence. The wind 'blew around' and grew heavier and colder at night. Then it finally blocked the channel, causing back and costal pain. These areas are the liver meridian's route."

According to her symptoms, I gave her the right needle prescription and methods to expel the external factors, and she felt immediately improved after treatment.

These conversations made me remember when I was twenty-four years old, I traveled to Mount Titlis of Switzerland with my husband on a sunny winter day. We took the cable car to the top of the mountain (3238 meters high, and the outside temperature was -30C). But we didn't feel cold with the heater in the cable car and the restaurant on the mountain. I was so excited that I opened the door and ran outside onto the glacier. I took five steps. I froze. Immediately I rushed back into the warm restaurant. It was freezing. But when we were inside the building, we couldn't feel or imagine how cold it was outside, because it looks the same, a sunny day!

External factors quickly invade us without our knowledge; the same elements can affect different people. Some get muscle aches, and some get headaches, get sore throats or back pain, and so on, depending on each person's physical weakness type. Once external factors invade our bodies, we need more energy to repair ourselves, and thus we feel unusually sleepy and tired. We need more rest, a light diet, lots of water, and sound sleep for a good recovery in this situation.

One of the reasons that hospitalized patients recover rapidly is that their busyness is removed to take time to lie in bed, sleep, and recharge. Refraining from sexual activity is also an essential factor for recovery. From the TCM perspective, sexual behavior consumes a lot of kidney energy, which the body needs and a lack of power affects restoration. So Chinese medicine practitioners suggest that people should be abstinent when they are sick. Once we know what causes the symptoms, we know better ways to prevent them.

In another case, during Christmas, one of my female patients strongly invited me to have a light lunch at her house to show her appreciation for my treatments. When I entered her lovely home, I immediately noticed her windows were open. And when I hugged her, both of her hands felt cold. So I said, "Hey, lady, your hands are cold. Why don't you close your windows and wear more?"

She replied, "We should open the windows to let the house ventilate well, right? That's what we did in our homeland. Didn't you?"

I said, "Yes, you are right; I did that before too. But actually, we'd adapt to local conditions. For example, it's winter now, so I turned on the heater in my clinic and my house to keep warm. But you haven't turned on the heater and, on the contrary, you are opening all the house windows! It's too cool and windy! No wonder you are visiting me every week for treatments. You get invaded by the wind cold often."

My favorite herbal dish for the common cold

This is a dish I often cook for myself and my children to treat common colds or general weakness: a simple noodle soup.

1. Boil slices of ginger for fifteen minutes, add thin noodles, and cook for a few minutes until well-cooked.
2. Before turning off the stove, add a generous a mount of chopped green onions and cilantro/coriander.
3. Add a little salt and white pepper on top and eat it while it's warm.
4. Some may sweat a little afterward.
5. Get a full night's rest after finishing the meal, we feel much better the next day.

Same Virus but Variable Symptoms

Know thyself, ever-victorious.
Know thyself and thou shalt know the world.

Ancient axiom

Treat the same disease with a different formula.
Treat different diseases with the same formula.

In 2020, we experienced a serious viral outbreak that affected the whole planet, COVID-19. How do we, as TCM/OM doctors, diagnose this? It's an "Epidemic of Dampness Toxin". For thousands of years, Asia has had more than four hundred epidemics during history and has created a complete system through accumulated experiences in its application of control, treatment, and prevention against outbreaks or pandemics.

This "Epidemic of Dampness Toxin" is a highly contagious and infectious disease that can infect people of all ages. Fever, sore throat, fatigue, body aches, dry cough, abdominal pain, and loss of smell/taste are the main symptoms, but the symptoms themselves can vary widely from person to person. We have seen some people who are experienced skin rashes too. However, some people do not show any symptoms. A small number of patients may develop severe complications or even die with Acute Respiratory Distress Syndrome (ARDS). Long-term damage of Covid-19 showed: liver/kidney disease, brain fog, memory loss, difficulty focusing, sleep problems, fatigue, and more. The effects can range from mild to severe.

Our ancestral doctors classified pathogens into different "exterior factors", calling them "evils" (外邪: wind, cold, fire, heat, dryness, dampness, and even toxin) based on the different symptoms they caused. People with varying constitutions of the body are susceptible to various external factors. We believe that each microorganism's survival, reproduction, and spread require specific suitable environmental conditions. For example, enterovirus and dengue fever occur in summer, related to heat and fire "evil pathogenic external factors. Some viruses that happen in winter are related to cold and damp "evil" pathogenic external factors. We reflexively adjust the human body's response to the diseases, including antiviruses, to help the body's immune response. Not directly work on the virus or bacteria itself.

For example, we can pretend that there are a lot of cockroaches and ants in my kitchen. Instead of self-reflecting on whether it should be cleaned and kept clean so that these insects won't appear, I kill them with insecticides and the environment -my kitchen- is still not clean and therefore suitable for the bugs' growth; they will continue to appear in my kitchen.

I love this quote from the book: "The Biology of Belief"- by Bruce H. Lipton, Ph.D.

Cells as miniature humans, when cells get sick, think of the environment. Organisms adapt to their environment and can pass on those adaptations to future generations. The genes we inherit from our mother and our father are not our fate. It's the environment!

TCM/OM doctors give treatment according to syndrome differentiation, and based on the patient's physical constitution: deficiency, excess, dampness, cold, heat, and the strength of the patient's righteous "qi" ; then they prescribe the treatment. The doctors should always know to accommodate three factors: each person's constitution, location, and climate. From the perspective of five thousand years of history, herbal formulas provide people with harmonious immunity and promote better immunity during an epidemic. (Consult your TCM/OM physician to develop a herbal supplement to help you based on your body constitution.)

Now, let's first get a sense of the terms "Yin" and "Yang." Simply speaking, "Yin" refers to the tangible substance, such as blood, body fluids, muscle, and tissue; it's material. At the same time, "Yang" is the intangible energy of the body, including "qi,". Yin and Yang move and cooperate to maintain bodily functions. Yin and Yang's overall homeostasis makes up what we call an individual's "body constitution". For example, people with insufficient Yang are vulnerable to "wind, cold, and dampness" while those with deficient Yin are vulnerable to "dryness, heat, and wind." Those with poor Yin, Yang, qi, and blood function are prone to "dampness" and related diseases. Also, people with different body constitutions need to pay attention to other things regarding medication and diet. Eating food with cool properties, such as watermelon, might make people with Yang deficiencies weaker. People with a Yin deficiency should avoid food with hot properties, such as spicy chili and fried foods, or they may generate too much inner heat. Inappropriate food therapy will cause an imbalance in the body's Yin and Yang and increase susceptibility to infectious diseases.

That's why the same diseases can have wildly variable symptoms from person to person. It depends on each person's body constitution, mind, and spiritual state; it's very personalized.

Human beings are just like exquisite computers built with software and hardware. TCM/Oriental Medicine as an "Energy Medicine" works well with the human body's software, programming, and healing capabilities are no longer a mystery. Our advanced human technology has succeeded in measuring the Qi effect. Now we have tools to measure the Qi and the twelve meridians in their balanced state.

In any case, combining the knowledge and treatment methods of modern Western medical science with ancient Eastern healing ways is an excellent way to fight the epidemic and seek all humankind's generous welfare—unity to victory.

Four Seasons & Twenty-Four Seasons

We are little parts living on this planet, so, of course, we are connected to the environment and climate.

Dr. Jessie Lee

In mid-April, after spring break and Easter, my son asked me, "How come this spring and summer is so strange? Isn't it supposed to be hot by Easter? Why is it cold like winter these days? The temperature is chilly, and the mountains are snowy. This climate is so weird!"

I responded, "Remember I always said that after May 5th, which is the Dragon Boat Dumpling Festival on the Lunar Calendar, we can pack the winter clothes and take out the summer clothes. Summer officially begins after the Dragon Festival. You will see."

On June 7th, I received a message from my daughter from Portland, Oregon, asking, "Mom, did we just pass a new season according to the twenty-four seasons thing? Because both my roommate and I have been very sleepy for no reason lately…"

"Super! Your body is reacting correctly and synchronizing with the climate. Just yesterday, we left one of the twenty-four seasons called mángzhòng 芒种, the ninth solar term," I told her.

The mángzhòng 芒种 or "Seeding Grain" season is a typical summer climate, which predicts that the weather will start to get hot. There is a farmer's saying: "If there is a thunderstorm within these two weeks, it is a good harvest year!" During this time, you can see watermelons, mangoes, pineapples, and other tropical fruits. Also, the flowering period of many flower species has expired at this time, so it is rare to see a large number of butterflies migrating and eating pollen.

The earliest complete records of the twenty-four seasons appear in the Western Han Dynasty (BC 179-122), a masterpiece <Huai Nanzi 崔南子-Astronomical Training>, clearly recording the name and sequence of the twenty-four solar terms, which is still being used today. Twenty-four solar terms point out the periodic law of climate change in a year. It is the ancient people's practical wisdom who used photogrammetry at the height of astrology and nature. It results in a "weather communication and forecasting table." Since ancient times, it has helped the Chinese people who rely on agriculture to expect the climate changes of nature, expected rainfall, and frost length. It has indeed provided an essential reference for farmers' sowing and farming for millennia.

The twenty-four seasons begin from the vernal equinox. Every fifteen degrees is a solar term, and each solar term is about half a month. Although most modern people are unfamiliar with this calendar, the 5Y6Q theory used as a theoretical framework in Chinese medicine uses this calendar. The ancients discovered that natural climate change would impact human health; when the climate changes abnormally or is unbalanced, it will cause disease.

In the ancient medical book Yellow Emperor's Classic of Internal Medicine Huangdi Neijing 黃帝內經, there are many discussions on the importance of climate change on human health. Whenever solar energy replaces the period, it is like an aircraft's turbulent instability in high winds, causing the body to need more power to synergize and balance fluctuating temperatures and changes. Often one feels unusually sleepy or tired.

From the perspective of TCM, summer is the time for sweating and detoxification. In winter, it is necessary to keep warm and to store energy. This is the most natural healthy living philosophy. Still, the large-scale use of modern air-conditioning systems in closed room spaces makes our respiratory system fragile. It makes us lose our understanding of the natural seasons and our innate sensitivity to temperature. It is no wonder that we TCM practitioners always ask people to use air conditioners less and avoid icy drinks to avert health damage.

The Yin-Yang and the four seasons are the roots of everything. The sages cultivate Yang in spring and summer, and they conserve Yin in fall and winter to follow the basic principle of preserving health. According to the universal law, "engendering in Spring, growing in Summer, reaping in Autumn, and storing in Winter."

From a micro of a year to a day, or a macro of a lifetime, it's the same pattern. Active during the daytime- spring, summer; and rest during the nighttime- fall, and winter.

We can't stop the change of seasons, we can't stop getting old, but we can be wise gardeners and arrange the gardens to be colorful and lush according to the seasons.

Note

Most sicknesses are related to the Four seasons/Four energies. "Don't be a person who digs a well when one is thirsty, or casts the weapon after the war has already broken out." Chapter two, On Preserving Health. Yellow Emperor. Chinese seasons are based on observations of the sun and stars. Many Chinese calendrical systems have started the new year on the second new moon after the winter solstice.

Twenty Four Seasons

The Yin-Yang and the four seasons are the root of everything. The sages cultivate Yang in the spring and summer, and conserve Yin in autumn and winter in order to follow the basic principle of preserving health; it is in accordance with the universal law, "Engendering in Spring, growing in Summer, harvest in Autumn, and storing in Winter."

Four seasons / four energies in a day:

Spring	Morning	7:00AM - 1:00PM
Summer	Noon	1:00PM - 7:00PM
Autumn	Evening	7:00PM - 1:00AM
Winter	Night	1:00AM - 7:00AM

Four seasons / four energies in a lifetime:

Spring	1 year old - 25 years old
Summer	25 years old - 50 years old
Autumn	50 years old - 75 years old
Winter	75 years old - 100 years old

Yang Seasons

Spring

立春	Beginning of Spring	*lìchun*
雨水	Rain Water	*yushui*
驚蟄	The Waking of Insects	*jingzhé*
春分	The Spring Equinox	*chunfen*
清明	Pure Brightness	*qingming*
谷雨	Grain Rain	*guyu*

Summer

立夏	Beginning of Summer	*lixià*
小滿	Small Grain	*xiaoman*
芒種	Grain In Ear	*mángzhòng*
夏至	The Summer Solstice	*xiàzhì*
小暑	Minor Heat	*xiaoshu*
大暑	Major Heat	*dàshu*

Ying Seasons

Autumn

立秋	Beginning of Autumn	*lìqiu*
處暑	The End of Heart	*chushu*
白露	White Dew	*báilù*
秋分	The Autumn Equinox	*qiufen*
寒露	Cold Dew	*hánlù*
霜降	Frost's Descent	*huangjiàng*

Winter

立冬	Beginning of Winter	*lìdong*
小雪	Lesser Snow	*xiaoxue*
大雪	Greater Snow	*dàxue*
冬至	The Winter Solstice	*dongzhì*
小寒	Minor Cold	*xiaohán*
大寒	Major Cold	*dàhán*

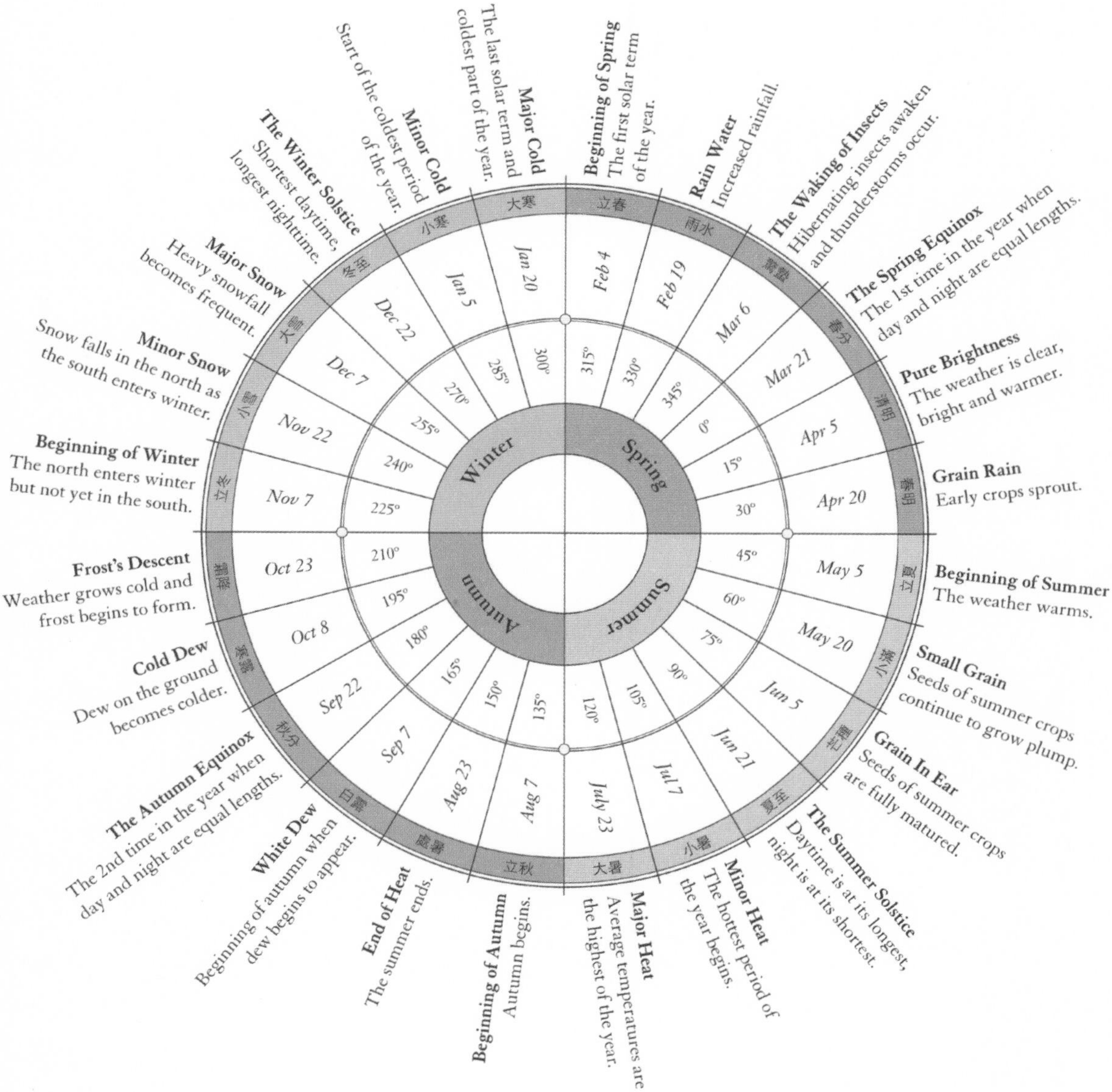
Winter
Spring
Summer
Autumn
Beginning of Spring
The first solar term of the year.
立春
Feb 4
315°
Rain Water
Increased rainfall.
雨水
Feb 19
330°
The Waking of Insects
Hibernating insects awaken and thunderstorms occur.
驚蟄
Mar 6
345°
The Spring Equinox
The 1st time in the year when day and night are equal lengths.
春分
Mar 21
0°
Pure Brightness
The weather is clear, bright and warmer.
清明
Apr 5
15°
Grain Rain
Early crops sprout.
穀雨
Apr 20
30°
Beginning of Summer
The weather warms.
立夏
May 5
45°
Small Grain
Seeds of summer crops continue to grow plump.
小滿
May 20
60°
Grain In Ear
Seeds of summer crops are fully matured.
芒種
Jun 5
75°
The Summer Solstice
Daytime is at its longest, night is at its shortest.
夏至
Jun 21
90°
Minor Heat
The hottest period of the year begins.
小暑
Jul 7
105°
Major Heat
Average temperatures are the highest of the year.
大暑
July 23
120°
Beginning of Autumn
Autumn begins.
立秋
Aug 7
135°
End of Heat
The summer ends.
處暑
Aug 23
150°
White Dew
Beginning of autumn when dew begins to appear.
白露
Sep 7
165°
The Autumn Equinox
The 2nd time in the year when day and night are equal lengths.
秋分
Sep 22
180°
Cold Dew
Dew on the ground becomes colder.
寒露
Oct 8
195°
Frost's Descent
Weather grows cold and frost begins to form.
霜降
Oct 23
210°
Beginning of Winter
The north enters winter but not yet in the south.
立冬
Nov 7
225°
Minor Snow
Snow falls in the north as the south enters winter.
小雪
Nov 22
240°
Major Snow
Heavy snowfall becomes frequent.
大雪
Dec 7
255°
The Winter Solstice
Shortest daytime, longest nighttime.
冬至
Dec 22
270°
Minor Cold
Start of the coldest period of the year.
小寒
Jan 5
285°
Major Cold
The last solar term and coldest part of the year.
大寒
Jan 20
300°

Cosmic Medicine,
Sixty Animals

Tis true without lying, certain most true;
That which is below is like that which is above.
As above, so below, as within, so without.

W.B. Yeats, Magus

I was on a South Bay coastal trip with Dr. Chi, Dr. Wang, and Dr. Liu, three of my peers from Five Branches University in California, when I heard the news that one of my beloved senior friends had recently acquired rectal cancer. I started talking to them about this. As I was going into detail, they said, "You don't need to tell us those symptoms now; we want to see his health issue in a bigger structure. Just give us his birthday."

I gave them his birthday. "According to the TCM astrology 'Wu Yun Liu Qi- Five Movements & Six Qi-5Y6Q'" we play a role in understanding a person's natural-born constitution. Your friend is sharp and smart and strong with high tolerance. His rectal cancer will be OK, not too dangerous for the time being..."

"The weak part of his health is Earth's motion, which is the spleen and stomach system. That's why he is susceptible to digestive and rectal problems when his body's energy is low or too stressed. Those symptoms were a chronic problem, but they became severe since winter of last year, and they turned into cancer eventually."

"He has to carefully manage his digestive and lung system, also his stress levels because when his energy of Earth is insufficient, the Wood-Wind energy will prevail on a large scale (Wood subjugates Earth.) The lung and large intestines share a parallel relationship, which means your friend should also take extra care of his respiratory system and allergies."

Baffled, I asked, "What are you guys talking about? How can you gather his health information from just his birthday? Is this a kind of fortune-telling? What is 'Wu Yun Liu Qi-Five Movements & Six Qi-5Y6Q?'"

Dr. Chi, my dissertation advisor, said,

"If the Yellow Emperor's Classic of Internal Medicine Huangdi Neijing is Chinese Medicine's crown, 'Wu Yun Liu Qi- Five Movements & Six Qi-5Y6Q' theory is the brightest centerpiece jewel."

With so much curiosity and hunger to learn, in 2016, I flew to New York a year later to attend a worldwide "Wu Yun Liu Qi 五運六氣 Five Movements & Six Qi-5Y6Q" training course, taught by the pioneer Dr. Xiao Mei Mao, the president of WFCMY (World Federation of Chinese Medicine YunQi Societies).

I saw the extraordinary documentary evidence from thousands of years ago, written by our ancestors. Knowing that over thousands of years, our ancestors observed and kept plentiful records of the movements of the five planets in our solar system: Jupiter, Mars, Saturn, Venus, and Mercury. Those planet's rotation patterns always keep in motion related to Earth's five elemental rules. The ancestors count with ten Gan Zhi[1] (Stem-Branch) every ten years with five different types: wood year, fire year, earth year, metal year, and water year. And each type has an "excessive year" in an "even" year and a "deficiency year" in a "singular" year. An excess year is followed by a deficiency year.

Besides, when the year's type appears, that year's climate has certain characteristics of that type. For example, the "fire" year has the characteristics of heat, the "water" year has the features of cold, and the "earth" year has the features of rain; the "metal" year has the features of dryness and the "wood" year has the features of wind. That's what we called Five Yun-5Y: Wood→Fire→Earth→Metal→Water.

These are the forces that balance nature. These balanced forces correct the weather changes on the earth and prevent excess/deficiencies that would lead to extinction. For example, when the weather changes too drastically in one year, these forces will ease the next year's changes. Only in this way can everything keep growing.

Then the ancients discovered needs to describe the complexity of the weather on top of 5Y; the 5Y can only describe the changing characteristics of the weather every "year," and for the more detailed weather changes within a year, the ancestors count with twelve Di Zhi[2] (Earthly Branches) the duodecimal to measure the smaller scale. So the ancients summed up the concept of six qi based on observation of celestial phenomena. That's what we called Six Qi-6Q: wind, cold, fire, heat, dryness, and dampness.

1. How do we mark and count those patterns? The Ganzhi 干支 (Stem-Branch) system combination is a unique way to mark time, days, and months, developed in the second millennium BC, during the Shang dynasty. As we humans have ten fingers, we use ten Heavenly Stems, 天 Tien 干 Gan, to count decimal periods, such as 甲 (jia, "first") 乙 (yi, "second") 丙 (bing, "third") 丁 (ding, "fourth") 戊 (wù, "fifth") 己 (ji, "sixth") 庚 (geng, "seventh") 辛 (xin, "eighth") 壬 (rén, "ninth") 癸 (gue, "tenth"), as an ordinal, used in similar contexts to Roman numerals in English numbering and outlining.

I was amazed by this pattern and immediately questioned, "Why is no one born in perfect balance? Why is there excess and deficiency?"

Then I realized immediately, of course, when you see it on the macro scale, it must work this way, in a bigger view of ten, thirty, and sixty years, all balanced. We all have our life lessons to learn and a mission to complete, and no one was born on this Earth perfectly. If you were perfect, you wouldn't be here on this Earth.

Therefore, 5Y6Q showed us the pattern of illness trends in the Earth cooperating with climate changes every year; the routine continues to rotate throughout the millennium. With this thousand-year pattern recorded, it helps us foresee epidemic disease years, the weather characteristics, ways to manage body health, and even human societal trends. Everybody's unique life and health data information connects with our specific birth date, as our code. We are part of the Earth, of course, so we are affected by changing weather and different universal influences.

This method is a pioneering technology for predicting human illness trends. (In this world, there are many other methods to predict personality or one's life blueprint, but this 5Y6Q is a study of illness.)

As a result, here are a total of ten types of body constitutions. Our ancestors used twelve animals of the zodiac to describe the twelve Earthly Branches so that ordinary people could more easily remember and understand them. These twelve signs of animals represent how we present and reflex ourselves: rat, ox, tiger, rabbit, dragon, snake, horse, goat, monkey, rooster, dog, and pig. There are similarities to the Western world's twelve astrological constellations.

No wonder I loved the Disney movie "Zootopia." We are like a big animal family globally, to understand, respect, and harmonize. That's why I always love to describe these sixty types of people as a happy zoo; no one is born perfect, but that's the lesson we need to learn: to know ourselves, to know others and all kinds of animals living together on this planet Earth.

According to the TCM Yellow Emperor's Classic of Internal Medicine Huangdi Neijing 黃帝內經 theory, every sixty years completes a sexagenary cycle, and a human's life expiration date is 120 years, two sexagenary cycles. With the first cycle, we learn of ourselves through sickness and mistakes and we make corrections. During the second cycle, if we acknowledge our problems and learn how to improve, we can live healthily and harmoniously until the last day of this life, which is around 120 years old.

Coincidentally, the Mayan interstellar calendar also has a similar calculation for life stream, but it focuses more on one's mission, challenge, talent, skills. The first round is 52 years, and then the second cycle till around 104 years old.

I learned to have the courage to recognize my weak and strong parts, improve shortcomings, appreciate my strengths, and tolerate my own limitations. I don't have to wait for scientific verification. I found that it is accurate and useful.

In the 2016 New York 5Y6Q course, I saw the world beyond the Earth, saw the movement of our solar system, saw how the Universe affects our health. I saw an immortal life. My energy and attention were one hundred percent fixed on ancient documentaries, natural beauty, disaster pictures, and the laws and rhythms of solar planetary operations. I saw how tiny we humans are on this Earth and within the Universe, but I also saw how the greatest power of the Universe has worked from beginning to end.

When I look at the large scale, I see the balancing of the Universe itself. When I saw a large scale of a thousand-year-long life stream, in an instant, I understood the importance of truly living in the moment. I felt the blood and energy of my ancestors running in my body and my soul. I'm not alone, and I'm immortal. Such as a seed sprouting into a tree that grows with sun and water, chopped down to be burned, or made into paper.

Nothing is "forever," but the greatest power of the Universe is forever. Supported by this power of the Universe, why do we fear? Why do we worry? We only have to know that for the body, getting sick, old, and dying are the laws of the Universe. At least those are the laws of the material world, but our spirit is forever. I surrender to that power, try to keep myself in balance, and try to build the harmony resonant with that power, and in that way, I am in heaven. I am united with the Universe.

The Emperor said, "Since ancient times, it is considered that the existence of man has depended upon the communications of the variation of Yin and Yang energies, thus, human life is based on Yin and Yang.

Chapter three of The Yellow Emperor's Classic of Internal Medicine Huangdi Neijing 黃帝內經

When we understand the health energy path with respect, it can help us and others to fully understand the health experience and self-healing potential. But we should also avoid using a single representation to explain our lives. Remember, the health energy path is just a light that guides us to understand the problem's key issues and how to self-heal. They can't explain who we really are. There are many Jessies, Jones, and Roberts in the world who may have the same birthday and zodiac, but there are always other factors such as family, culture, social roles, genetic inheritance, growth experience, ideological value, beliefs, and interests that will affect our respective health energy paths.

12 Earthly Branches Terms	12 Zodiacs	12 Months	12 "Double Hour"	12 Meridians
1. 子 (zi)	Rat 鼠 (shu)	November	23:00 -1:00	Gallbladder
2. 丑 (chou)	Ox 牛 (niú)	December	1:00 -3:00	Liver
3. 寅 (yín)	Tiger 虎 (hu)	January	3:00 -5:00	Lung
4. 卯 (mao)	Rabbit 兔 (tù)	February	5:00 -7:00	Large Intestine
5. 辰 (chén)	Dragon 龍 (lóng)	March	7:00 -9:00	Stomach
6. 巳 (sì)	Snake 蛇 (shé)	April	9:00 -11:00	Spleen
7. 午 (wu)	Horse 馬 (ma)	May	11:00 -13:00	Heart
8. 未 (wèi)	Goat 羊 (yáng)	June	13:00-15:00	Small Intestine
9. 申 (shen)	Monkey 猴 (hóu)	July	15:00-17:00	Urinary Bladder
10. 酉 (you)	Rooster 雞 (ji)	August	17:00-19:00	Kidney
11. 戌 (xu)	Dog 狗 (gou)	September	19:00-21:00	Pedicaldio
12. 亥 (hài)	Pig 豬 (zhu)	October	21:00-23:00	Triple Jiao

Note

The ancestor use twelve Di Zhi 地支 (Earthly Branches) the duodecimal to count, to represent: the (approximately) twelve years of Jupiter's orbital period, also representing the twelve months of the Chinese lunar year, and forming the twelve Chinese zodiacs and personified as twelve or sixty types known as sexagenary cycle 六 liu 十 shi 甲 jia 子 zi. Each branch has its literary name, such as: 子 (zi) 、丑 (chou)、寅 (yín)、卯 (mao)、辰 (chén)、巳 (sì)、午 (wu)、未 (wèi)、申 (shen)、酉 (you)、戌 (xu)、亥 (hài) and the duodecimal divisions of the day into "double hours," beginning with 11:00 pm, formed by TCM's twelve meridians circadian clock.

Color Legend

◼	Excess Earth	◼	Deficient Earth
◼	Excess Metal	◻	Deficient Metal
◼	Excess Water	◼	Deficient Water
◼	Excess Wood	◼	Deficient Wood
◼	Excess Fire	◼	Deficient Fire

Chinese Zodiac

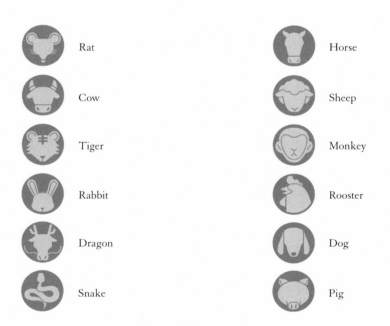

🐀	Rat	🐎	Horse
🐂	Cow	🐑	Sheep
🐅	Tiger	🐒	Monkey
🐇	Rabbit	🐓	Rooster
🐉	Dragon	🐕	Dog
🐍	Snake	🐖	Pig

Birth Year Element, Zodiac, Tweleve Branch Relationship Chart

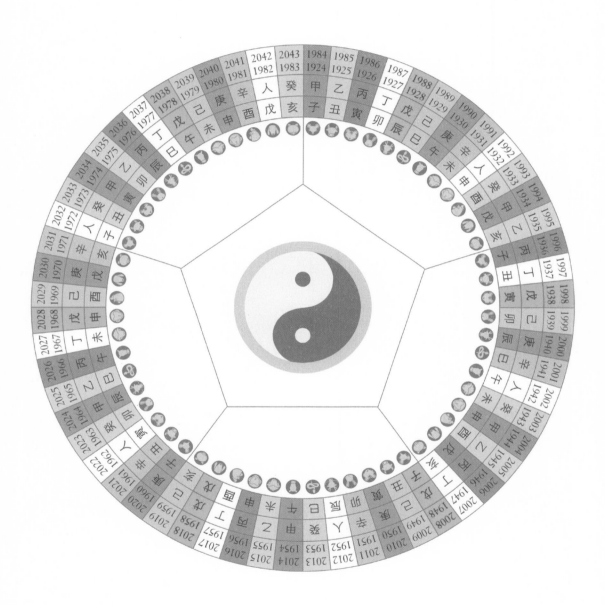

Even years are excess years, odd years are deficiency years, see example below:

Even Years		**Odd Years**	
1960	Metal excess	1965	Metal deficiency
1962	Wood excess	1967	Wood deficiency
1964	Earth excess	1969	Earth deficiency
1966	Water excess	1961	Water deficiency
1968	Fire excess	1963	Fire deficiency

Elemental Compatibility

Water nourishes wood;
Wood fuels fire;
Fire enriches earth;
Earth produces metal;
Metal guides water.

Elemental Incompatibility

Water extinguishes fire;
Fire melts metal;
Metal chops down wood;
Wood drains earth;
Earth stagnates water.

Five Elements Relationship Chart

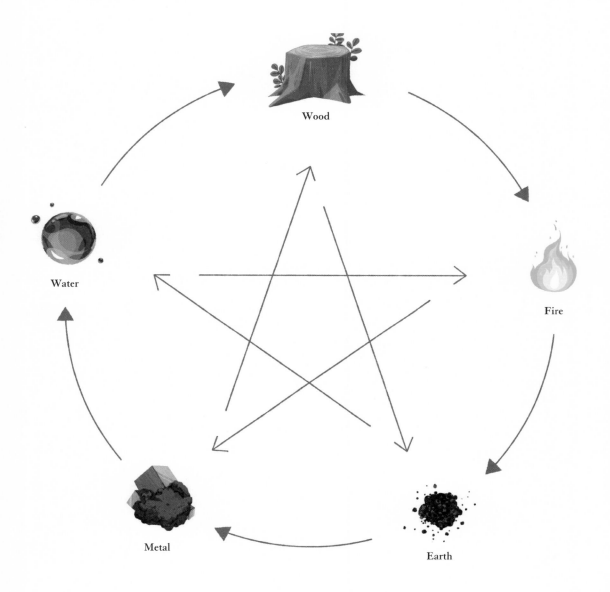

Wood

Water

Fire

Metal

Earth

Into Energy Medicine

When the frequency is right, life is right. Discover the energy rhythm of your body, mind, and spirit, and work with its resonance.

Dr. Jessie Lee

As I have mentioned before, after my only brother died in a violent shooting, my mom began her five years of healing her severe depression. Most of the time, she lived with me in Los Angeles, so I experienced all of Mom's suffering during that period.

I believe that people who have lived with sick and elderly family members or depressed people for a long while have a deeper understanding of suffering as they are also affected by these illnesses. I often went with my mother's ups and downs. The negative energy would strongly affect my emotions and health state. I knew I needed to calm myself down, but that is easier said than done. At that time, I was healing from Barrett's esophagus with dysplasia, going through a divorce, raising three children alone, studying as a full-time student of oriental medicine, and spending three months focusing all my energy preparing for my license exam. The pressures of life make one's health a lot more challenging.

One day, I went to a friend's house to ask some questions about tax issues. It was customary to have the air conditioning on during the hot summer. At that time, I hadn't learned to protect myself from direct cold winds, so I began to get a stuffy nose after some discussion. I ignored that symptom, thinking it was a reaction to the cold air, and I believed after I left the house, the warm temperature outside could have helped open my nasal congestion, and I was able to breathe normally.

But unexpectedly, while driving back home on the freeway, my nose didn't get any better. On top of that, I was having difficulty breathing. I suddenly looked at my hand and fingers on the steering wheel. My nails were purple, it immediately alarmed me. Then I looked at the rear view mirror and saw that my face and lips were also pale and purple. I knew the situation wasn't right: something was wrong with my heart blood circulation. Myocardial infarction? Heart failure causing a blood circulation blockage?

Oh my God, oh my God! I was thinking,

"This is a terrible situation. I better stop driving and call an ambulance for help."

I slowed down my car and planned to stop at the shoulder on the freeway to call for an ambulance. While I was heading for the shoulder, I took out a pen and jabbed it hard into my left HT5 Neiguan 內關 point, located inside the left arm. This point is good for helping the heart, chest, and stomach in emergencies, as the left arm is closest to our heart. After about fifteen seconds, I was able to take a big breath. It worked! So I kept pressing all the pericardium and heart meridians on the left arm while continuing to take deep breaths. My whole body was screaming,

"Need oxygen! Need oxygen! Hurry!!!"

After a few deep breaths, as the car was about to stop on the shoulder, a dramatically thought came to me:

"No, I can't stop here now. If I call an ambulance and go to the hospital, the cold environment there will freeze me to death, and if they rescue me with electric shocks to my heart, I am sure my ribs will break since I am so thin, and I don't have money for an emergency. It's horrible! "

This thought terrified me, so I took a chance at getting home while breathing and pressing the HT5 Neiguan 內關 point. I told myself to drive home; my daughter was there, and she could help me get my acupuncture needles. So I turned the car away immediately, returning to the freeway and heading home.

While driving, I kept using the pen to stimulate the acupuncture points. With three exits left to get home, I suddenly remembered my doctor friends from school. Their acupuncture clinic was in the next exit area. I decided to go to their clinic to get help, and if they weren't there, I'd go home to find my daughter.

I immediately got off the freeway and drove into the clinic. As I approached the traffic lights at the corner, I prayed anxiously, "No, no, no, please don't turn red, I am in an emergency...I'm dying...Please...!"

Fortunately, I was lucky to get to the clinic in three minutes. I rushed in and shouted to my doctor friends, "Emergency! Emergency!"

"Emergency? You have to wait; the clinic room is full now," my friend said, amused. He thought I was joking.

But when he looked at me closer, he noticed it was a bad situation and immediately led me into his office. He used the OPT tuina technique to rescue me by pressing the upper back scapular region, the TCM version of CPR. Then he asked, "What happened? Your face is so pale, and your lips are purple. Are you okay?"

After a few minutes of OPT CPR tuina, my breathing became smoother. When the treatment table was available, my friends helped me lie down, put two needles on the HT5 Neiguan 內關 point, and rest.

It's no exaggeration. As soon as I lay down, I quickly resumed breathing without any pain. After about fifteen minutes, I took out the needles by myself and got off the treatment table. Then I lifted the sheets because I wanted to know which brand of the table I was lying on. I had never experienced a table that was so warm, relaxing, and comfortable… I was curious.

My doctor friend happened to enter that room just then. He asked,

"Hey! Did you take out your needles? Are you better now?"

I replied, "I am completely okay now. Thank you so much, but I am quite curious about this warm mattress you are using for this treatment table? It's comfortable, calming and special."

And this was the first time I learned of a crystal amethyst mattress. After my friend introduced me to the functions, I said, "The price is not low, but if it has a good effect on treatment, I will buy it, and my mom can try it out first. You know she has been sick for many years. And if it helps, when I open my clinic, I will also be equipped with this to benefit patients."

Two weeks later, the crystal amethyst mattress came into my house, and I had my mom sleep on it every day. According to the book Shen Nong's Herbs recorded 3000 years ago, mineral stones such as crystals and tourmaline were used as medicines. They have the effect of calming the nerves, mind, anxiety, and sleep problem, the warmth helping with Yang deficiency type of person's poor circulation and body cold symptoms. (The same, as I mentioned in the previous chapter, it depends on each person's body type; the Yin deficiency with inner heat person might feel uncomfortable with this warm crystal mattress.)

My mother suffered from severe depression for over five years, and she had a Yang deficiency, the body often cold with a lousy appetite, and was unable to defecate properly. If there is not enough food in one's body, there is nothing to convert into energy. Without energy, the overall metabolic system weakens and worsens. When there are insufficient nutrients and energy to promote brain function, it becomes more hypoxic, so there are symptoms of dementia in the elderly who do not maintain a healthy, balanced diet and digestive system. It's a vicious cycle.

The warm crystal amethyst mattress combines two important life elements to help people return to health: the first is warm energy, which drives circulation by gentleness. The effect of crystals clearing the nerves strengthens the role of parasympathetic nerves. People can sleep deeply at night; the body can sufficiently repair itself in a deep sleep. The recovery function of the digestive and circulatory systems and the overall qi and blood are smooth. The human intestines are closely related to the brain's cerebral ileum, and healing the intestines can also help our brain system return to normal. It was a "miracle" that unfolded before my eyes.

One week after my mother used the warm crystal mattress, she told me happily that she had many bowel movements with good form. It seemed to clean her old sputum. On that same day, I found that my mother had regained her appetite and wanted to eat. After two weeks, she ate as much food as me; a month later, she began to leave the house and walk around the park happily to sunbath. After three months, her depression had nearly completely vanished.

Scalp needling helped restore my mom's memory, while the crystal warming helped her five-year depression. When my mother was planning her trip to Germany to visit my elder sister, I told my sister on the phone,

"Mom is finally not looking for a cure on this trip to Europe, she is healthy and happy. She is going to visit you for a fun and to enjoyable summer in Europe."

My curiosity about energy medicine has grown, thanks to the calming effect and unique energy of the minerals and crystals that came into my life. It made me decide to take three additional years of a doctoral program to continue my studies in the energy medicine field. While telling this story, I was still so moved with gratitude! The incredible energy of this world!

Natural Healing Journey

Spirit Medicine

Everything can be our medicine
including the spirit; If we know how to
use it correctly, it can help us obtain a
healthy and happy life.

Dr. Jessie Lee

Though I took Guided Meditation in my psychology class in 2005, it would be another twelve years before meeting someone who also knew this healing technique. In 2016, my partner and I decided to start up a new acupuncture clinic. After nearly half a year of searching around, I finally signed a five-year contract at a location near a beautiful university town. We took an additional three months to remodel the clinic.

My partner was supposed to help buy the remodeling materials, such as flooring, lumber, cabinets, paint, curtains, and some other things. I ended up doing all that by myself, though. My partner had personal issues that he had to deal with first, which affected our remodeling plan. While at first this disappointed me, but then I was quite proud of myself and my accomplishment after finishing the project.

I felt that I had been more efficient in making my own decisions than I would have been working with my partner. However, the inner rationality and sensibility of the self still needed time to balance out. From time to time, I always felt some anger towards him even though I understood his situation, but I also knew I'd better find some way to let my rage become balanced. I hastened to ask for help from my counselor and made an appointment to see her. And, finally, I have reunited with Guided Meditation again after twelve years.

One day during this period, I walked into her office, telling her about several things. She thought for a few minutes and said, "The fact is that your clinic contract has been signed for five years, so you'd better move forward, you have to move on. Now you're in a partnership with a colleague who does nothing, yet you need an assistant. It seems that it is an awkward situation. It's time for you to meet your power animal."

I was suspicious but asked excitedly, "What? Power animal?"

She said, "You will know when you follow my instructions.

"Now, please follow my instructions. Close your eyes, let's take four deep breaths. Call on your physical self, emotional self, psychological self, and spiritual self all together.

"As you relax, you find yourself at a beach. It is safe and comfortable. Please describe the beach to me.

"In your inner vision, you begin to see a stair and slowly go downstairs to the ground. You find yourself looking at green grasses and distant trees. And then, you see a cave half-concealed behind a hill. You step carefully into the muted darkness of the inner cave. It's safe. When I count from one to three, you will find yourself already in the cave. One...Two...."

"Don't force it. Allow it to show itself to you. And as it does, its eyes seek you out and hold your gaze."

I followed the guidance, I saw it, a pair of brown-orange gleaming eyes calling my attention. And then slowly I saw its head. Wow! It was a black panther, elegant, alert but friendly, walking towards me slowly. Is that you? My power animal? I have always thought it may be a dog or cat. It was amazing!

After this Guided Meditation session, I will never forget how I felt when I stepped out of the office into the beautiful night and drove my car on the freeway; I thought I saw the black panther running dynamically by my car all the way home with me.

I moved with joy. I kept sending back gratitude to the people who have helped me and the universe; this is how the universe works with people; we are all connected, and we only need to reconnect with it to get help and guidance.

As I claimed the panther's power, I did have a lot of inner strength flow up in me, and I hastened to start running my new business alone.

Later on in life, while taking the National Guild Hypnotism training class, the teacher used guided meditation skills to lead us in "Age Regression," and I was surprised to see my four-year-old self. I saw my childhood self taking a nap and waking up at dusk. No one was around. I began to feel afraid and tense. I climbed out of bed and went out to the garden to find someone, but no one was at home. My father, mother, sisters, and brother were all gone.

It frightened me, and I climbed the wall alone, passed the spiked iron spires, and came to the street. I didn't know where to find my family, so I was anxiously standing on the road and crying.

Then two American missionary ladies who lived in front of my church home passed by on bicycles. They took me back to their home, put me in a beautiful American style dress, and told me not to be afraid, that Mom and Dad would come back soon, and that I could stay at their house. The two kind ladies took good care of me and baked the most delicious biscuits for me. Their home was full of American-style furniture, soft church music, lively green plants in the corner, and soft, warm interior lighting. Everything comforted me. My fear and anxiety disappeared. I stopped crying, and I was thrilled at their home.

I saw myself that when they sent me back home at night, I smugly showed a packet of biscuits to my sisters and said to them, "You see, I have these delicious biscuits, and I won't give them to you. I don't want to share with you, because you abandoned me and left me home alone! So horrible!"

The teacher asked, "Think slowly. Did that event influence your life?"

Yes! I am fifty years old now, and finally, I know why I'm always afraid to be alone during nighttime. I have to have my pets' or family's company. Otherwise, I will stay awake all night and be unable to sleep. No wonder I've adopted stray dogs since age five. I'm sure it was after that incident – I was afraid to be alone, so I insisted on having a dog or cat. The pets wouldn't leave me; I believe in their loyalty, they wouldn't let me down.

And since that incident, I became an interior decorator in my family, always setting up some plants, flowers, cozy pillows on the chair with warm light in our small, simple chapel house. I remembered once my mom wondered, " Where do you learn how to decorate the house? No one in the family does this. "

I called my elder sister after class, who is living in Germany, and said,

"Could you believe what I have seen in my hypnosis class? I saw four-year-old me in our hometown..."

My sister didn't let me finish and said,

" I know what happened…" Her description was accurate with what I have seen in my inner vision in the class. I happily said," So, it was true! It's not my imagination!"

It was another incredible journey of guided meditation. Now, I got some answers about the origins of my fear. Once we can identify the head of a constant emotion, it was fear of loneliness – then we can start to heal and embrace the inner child. The black panther came to support my healing. It gave me its nature: night-action power and silent patience; my internal weakness became stronger and stronger when I realized its special forces. Finally, after two weeks, I overcame my fear of being alone at night. It healed forty-six years of unknown fear.

Adapt & Transform: The Art of Self-Healing

Crystal Healing

I love myself, therefore, I live completely
in the now, experiencing each moment as
much as possible and knowing that my
future is bright and joyous and secure for
I am a beloved child of the Universe, and
the Universe lovingly takes care of me now
and forevermore. All is well in my life.

Louise Hay

One day, after an exhausting busy day at work, my cervical spondylosis pain came back. I was in a lot of pain, but I was too tired to put needles in myself. I just wanted a gentler, smoother treatment.

After dinner, I went into my room, closed the door, and lit up some candles. I burn some sage to smudge and let the smoke purify my energy. I meditated:

"The energy of the East, please enlighten me. The energy of the South, please strengthen me. The energy of West, please inform me. The energy of the North, please transform me. The father of the upper universe empowers me, the mother of the earth below supports, nutrients me. I am grateful."

Then, after three minutes of meditation, I took out an obsidian stone and held it in my left hand near my heart. Closing my eyes, I waited for the obsidian to start the healing process. After a few seconds, though, it still hadn't moved at all.

I was confused and said, "Hey, that's weird! Why didn't it move?"

Suddenly it dawned on me that I had forgotten to "give the order."

Okay, let's repeat 4-4-4-4 breathing to summon each level of myself: "Physical, Emotional, Psychological, and Spiritual self come together now. Please, obsidian, help me to heal my neck pain and shoulder pain."

In about three to five seconds, the obsidian stone started the healing process. My left hand, which held the obsidian, immediately began moving gently. I gradually followed the wave of energy up and down, sometimes tapping my shoulder and neck. Sometimes it is up to the body to sort out the chaotic star corpuscle energy; following this energy movement, the natural swing of the smooth energy wave, the obsidian took me dancing with its energy's flow.

After about twenty minutes, my whole body was warm, and my pain had decreased from an eight to a three out of ten. After a time, the movement gradually halted, everything returning to quiet.

Whether it is because of the movements' actions, which promote circulation and clear the pain of blockage, or because the invisible energy cleans up the subtle negative energy and relieves the pain, either way, it is helpful. At least I could sleep better that night without the pain affecting my quality of sleep.

Another sunny autumn afternoon, a fifty-five-year-old patient came to the clinic to continue her chronic rheumatoid arthritis treatment. But on that day, she didn't look the same as usual. She appeared absent-minded, and I supposed she was probably worried about something. The patient did not want to talk more, so I began acupuncture and moxibustion treatment on her.

At the end of the one-hour treatment, as she was putting on her coat and preparing to leave, I still had the feeling something was wrong with her. I had to ask:

"What's wrong, are you okay? Is there anything bothering you?"

She looked around making sure there is no one around, then whispered to me:

"I went to court yesterday for some family issues and saw a bunch of upsetting things there. I even saw the police strongly force a young boy to the back. That scene scared me! Then, when I walked out of the court, I got lost and couldn't find my car. It took me a while to remember where my car was."

"No wonder you look different. Today you are acting really out of character; you're traumatized from yesterday's shock. Let me use crystal energy to help you to relax."

I asked her to stand up, close her eyes, relax, and just count from one to ten. I held my white crystal and placed it fifteen centimeters from her chest, and gave the order: "Please use your energy to heal this frightened heart and help this woman recover her calm and peace."

After five minutes of the crystal healing process, finally, she felt herself calm down. She smiled and left.

Commonly Used Crystals

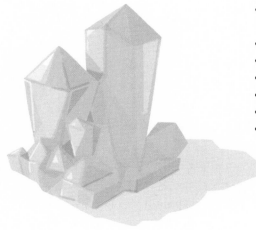

Quartz

- Considered a master healing crystal and the most versatile stone for healing and spiritual work.
- Amplifies the energies of other healing stones.
- Stimulates the immune and circulatory systems.
- Aids in concentrations and memory retention.
- Protects and balances the aura and all chakras.
- Bring mental strength and clarity.
- Cleanses the soul.

Black Obsidian

- Repels negative thoughts.
- Shields against negative energies.
- Draws out mental stress and tension.
- Combats emotional blockage and traumas.
- Promotes compassion and strength.
- Increases self-control
- Adjusts imbalances.

Purple Amethyst

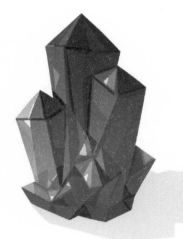

- Calms the mind.
- Helps with sleep.
- Attracts positive energy.
- Removes negative energy from the area.
- Promotes the parasympathic nervous system.
- Reduces feelins of stress, anxiety, and depression
- Procides spiritual protection and inner strength.
- Promotes a clear mind.

Yellow Crystals

- Promotes confidence.
- Boosts success in finances.
- Awakens, enlightens and adds optimism.
- Boosts sucess in new efforts, beginnings, and projects.
- Provides heightened awareness towards others.
- Increases alertness towards the environment.
- Helps with better communicaion and organization.
- Helps with new relationships.

Light Therapy

"We know today that man, essentially, is a being of light."

"We are still on the threshold of fully understanding the complex relationship between light and life, but we can now say emphatically that the function of our entire metabolism is dependent on light."

"All-natural organisms emit light energy at the cellular level, and that all organic life absorbs light and processes it internally. Faint, color-coded broadcasts of the light energy that cells emit are the basis of intercellular communication in all living organisms."

Dr. Fritz Albert Popp

The passion for healing for myself, family, friends, and patients inspired me to continue studying and doing research in the Oriental Medicine Doctorate program's energy medicine field.

In 2014, during a full moon in a short trip visit to my sister in Mexico City, I suddenly woke up at 2:00 AM thinking of my mom's treatment protocol. While looking out the window, my eyes fully attracted and focused on the bright round moon, ignoring the dark sky around it. Completely attracted by the bright light, I felt my whole being float and fly towards the light. It seemed I would go through its bright circle and enter another space. What is this space? Again...Who am I?

Suddenly, it was like I had awoken from a deep dream. I said to myself,

"Oh! I understand the meaning now of Matthew 6:33 'Seek first the kingdom of God, and His righteousness, and He shall add all these things unto you.'" I want to connect the phrase with OM as God refers to spirit, Yang, and unconscious mind. "All these things" refer to physical health, Ying, and material wealth.

If this dark, vast universe represents the world of "Yin" - the material world, my earthly self, then would the other end of this light be the kingdom of "Yang" - the energy, the higher self? Yin and Yang, a wholeness, the unity of the earthly me and the higher self, the unity of man and God? When my conscious mind is in the present, it means my thoughts are in the material world. The conscious mind's natural tendency is to take, desire, and crave, making us want more and more. Therefore, to be in balance, we look on the other side of "Yin," which is "Yang," or the subconscious mind, the energy program field, to expand, give, and share. Once we achieve an overall balance, we can enjoy a peaceful state.

I was talking to myself, "No wonder... Due to her son passing away and the severe depression this caused, Mom's health – her 'Yin and Yang' – are out of balance. The spiritual mind is equivalent to the Yang energy field. A Yang deficiency is causing low energy and body four limbs cold, which has slowed her metabolism, just like a falling Domino effect. Therefore, I should look for another side, to tonify Yang qi, to balance mom's health issues."

Therefore, on that cloudless, starry night, I realized many OM treatments include spiritual thinking. The material world is tangible; the body is solid; the Divine is intangible; the soul and the breath are invisible. We need to integrate the spiritual world of energy into our lives on earth to achieve integrity. And now, I realize that in the past fifty years, I have not deviated; I have always been walking in the Creator's path, to live my life in the universe's power, and to surrender in its energy guidance.

This thought made me feel full of joy and excitement. In the next few months, every time I saw patients in the clinic, I couldn't help but ask each one,

"What do you think when you see the moon in a cloudless, dark sky?"

During this time, many elderly patients and children frequently asked me, "Is there any acupuncture treatment that is used without needles? I am so afraid of needles!"

"What? Acupuncture without needles?" I said and scratched my head.

"Yes! Can you help us find out if there is any way to use needle-less acupuncture, but still with the effect of acupuncture meridian treatment?"

Endeavoring to help these patients, I began seriously researching and testing alternative methods for three years. Then I happened to discover Light Acupuncture, a treatment advocated by German Natural medical scientists and researchers. They found that light energy taken in visually could help with healing. Happily, I had an opportunity to take a class and obtain some clinical experience with Dr. Peter Mandel, one of the pioneers in the field.

I started to read many books on light energy and quantum mechanics. I remember complaining to my DAOM professor at the time, "I am studying a doctoral program of Oriental medicine and acupuncture, not physical science. Yet, I am reading so many books in that field."

Professor Chi "woke" me in a sentence, "Learning is to learn unknown things. If you already knew this stuff, then what would you be learning? You'd be wasting time."

It made sense. So I happily continue researching, surfing in quantum mechanics and the spectrum field.

Have you ever heard of someone who, at 2:30 AM, is moved to tears while reading physics, quantum mechanics, and physics textbooks? Well, that was me.

When I first saw the spectrum map, I learned that human vision is relatively narrow, and the range we can see with our eyes is limited. In quantum mechanics, the universe equals energy. Every element has its vibration. We are energy waves interacting with each other on the earth that touched my heart! Because I suddenly saw from the finite into infinite, from impermanence to eternal, that seeing required using our hearts, not optical vision. Life has no limitations, and we can choose not to let it trap us anymore. Therefore, Divine calm and peaceful energy flow quietly into everything we have, and we are "light." In this way, life becomes fascinating and free.

Each person is like a "light frequency," and acupuncture function relies on this "wave" we call Qi energy in the meridians to circulate throughout the body; it helps the body repair and recover itself, and restore the balance of Yin and Yang, like the unity of man and God.

In my research, I always do the first experiment on myself. So my first experience in light acupuncture was at the German clinic of Dr. Peter Mandel. The woman who received me first asked me to fill in some basic forms; then took me to the Kirlian energy emission analysis test. When I entered the doctor's office, the assistant had placed my profile and Kirlian report on the table. The doctor was reading the report and telling me all my physical health symptoms. I was stunned! That was very accurate.

Curious, I asked, "I know that you can see some of my present energy issues from the Kirlian report, but you haven't checked my pulse; how do you know my past health history and the symptoms of my internal organs?"

He replied, "Your Chinese I-Ching Hexagram has explained your life blueprint!"

On that day, he only put some needles in a few acupuncture points and then used a crystal light pen on those points. It took about twenty minutes. When I came down from the treatment table and walked on the ground, I suddenly asked my sister, who had accompanied me, "Hey! Is gravity still the same today?"

"What kind of question is that? Are you okay? Is something wrong with you? Of course, gravity is the same!" My sister replied.

"How can I be walking so lightly...As if my body were weightless! I feel like there is no gravity, and I am moonwalking. That's why I asked if anything had changed!"

The moonwalking sensation of lightness lasted for about five days. Not only was my body light, but my pains were also gone; my mood and mind were clear, calm, and peaceful. No wonder, for in some cases, light therapy helps with depression, bipolar, ADHD, and emotional disorder issues.

My cat, Dash, is an indoor/outdoor cat. One afternoon, I saw him come back from outside, and his paw was a bit strange. I checked carefully and found that his left paw was swollen to three times its normal size. It seemed like he had been stung by a bee. How could I treat him?

I immediately thought of light therapy and took out the device. Because I didn't need to touch Dash's body to administer the treatment, he was still and quiet. I used the anti-inflammatory blue light and the green light of regeneration on Dash for about eight minutes until he got up slowly to drink water, thus stopping the treatment.

Amazingly, after three hours, Dash's swollen paw was smaller! Wow! How could it be back to normal so quickly? It usually took three to five days for a bee sting to heal. Dash had recovered in a few hours.

My elder sister burned six centimeters of her skin while tending the fireplace at her home. It looked painful! While my sister was thinking about which herbs to apply, she suddenly thought about the light therapy that I was researching. Her experimental spirit woke up. She shone the blue light onto the burned wound while she watched a football game on TV. The wounded skin began aching in the first five minutes, then gradually transmitted burning pain to the shoulder's lymph nodes. After using the light for about ten minutes, she noticed the pain beginning to ease.

"Hey! It seems that it really works, the pain is lessening!" She told her husband.

My brother-in-law looked at the burnt patch of skin and said, "It must be very painful."

At that time, my sister was secretly saying: "Ha! It's getting less and less painful! Magical blue-light!"

That night, after watching TV and taking the blue light for about an hour, she eventually went to bed. The next day, the burn wound was not swollen or inflamed, and it had progressed rapidly toward healing.

Note
Burns are dominated by hydrogen, which is the red end of the spectrum. Using the property of oxygen at the blue end of the spectrum helps restore balance (1927 Atlanta Medical Journal Abstract).

The Seven Chakras

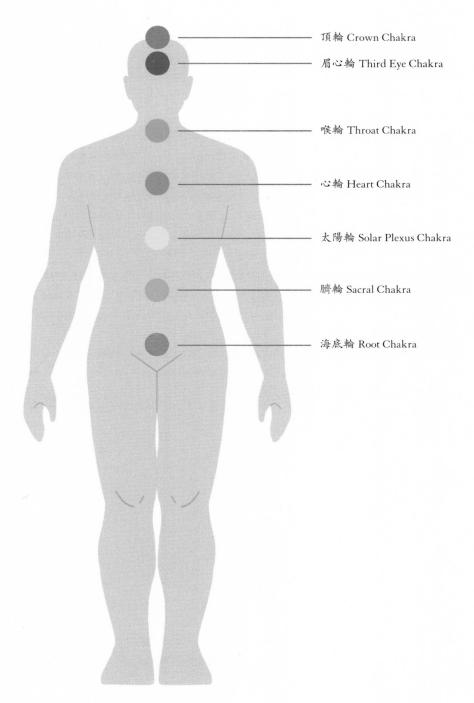

頂輪 Crown Chakra

眉心輪 Third Eye Chakra

喉輪 Throat Chakra

心輪 Heart Chakra

太陽輪 Solar Plexus Chakra

臍輪 Sacral Chakra

海底輪 Root Chakra

Spectrum of Light

Humans are only able to see a very small portion of the specturm of light, which we called visible light.

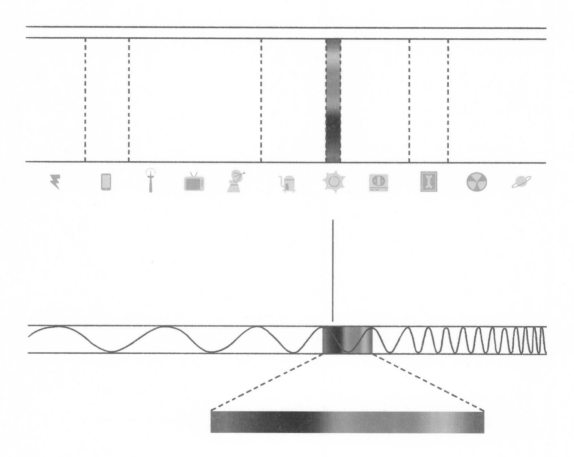

Clearing
& Resetting

Sometimes the hardest challenge for
ourselves is to look inside, to reflect, and to
change our life habits. Being sick gave me
this opportunity. I had to return to what
was simple, natural and sincere. Let's clear
and reset our data, lives and harvest.

Dr. Jessie Lee

When I am alone, whether I'm cooking or driving or doing housework or meditation, I always remember to clear my aka cord and clean up the junk database in my soul.

Clearing the junk not only helps me but my patients as well. Cleaning up my messy intangible web, which interfered with my health issues, helped me achieve a better life with joy. I use the ancient Hawaiian healing method Hooponopono: I am sorry, forgive me, thank you, I love you, which helps me clear my negative energy and emotions such as fear, anger, sadness, etc. (Referral book: Zero Limit by Joe Vitale)

Yes, I'm sorry that I let myself suffer in so many difficult situations; I am sorry that I put myself through those hard times. My experience has shown me that we are all connected, so I know I am responsible, especially when interacting with my patients, I do my best on my part, and patients have to do their part.

Forgive me for being so naive, and let myself carry all the burden for a long time.

Thank you for all of my dimensions and inner parts continuously to accompany me, helping release and clean out all my junk.

I love you (myself), yes; if I don't love myself, no one else will love me. And I love all parts of myself: my physical body and my emotional, psychological, and spiritual selves, my femininity and masculinity, my inner child, my higher self, my mother earth me, my subconscious and conscious me, and all.

Any of these emotions provide essential clues and lead me to heal internal wounds accumulating for a long, long time, sometimes even for hundreds or thousands of years.

In my opinion, humans are similar to sophisticated AI robots. The iPhone allows us to take pictures and record many things and then save these in the iCloud. But I believe that most people have not taken the time to sort out their photos and have even forgotten some of the pictures or videos taken: all of them were thrown into the iCloud memory, often exploding it past capacity.

Human beings can make many projections and links to the world through our five senses of sight, touch, hearing, smell, and taste and our actions, speech, and thoughts at any moment. Having such a huge storage capacity and connections can be burdensome, especially if we don't know how to organize or even delete these "junk files." But learning to "clear the data" will make us feel released from a heavy burden, and our mind will become more transparent, faster, and lighter once more. When your whole person is reset, you will feel like a new person with clarity.

My first experience of the benefits of clearing my unwated attachments, the aka cord, happened one day when I was fifty years old. My menopausal symptoms were severe: joint pain, fatigue, exhaustion, and mood swings. I quickly fell asleep while driving. My Western medicine health check noted hypothyroidism symptoms and related senescence of my endocrine and metabolic systems, which, according to Chinese Medicine, are related to the Qi and blood deficiencies of the kidney, liver, and spleen, and this is all part of the natural aging process. I saw myself as a plane experiencing turbulence; it's not forever; I told myself, I have to regain control of my body plane to go through the storm, and then life will go back to being peaceful.

Therefore, I was practicing the Clearing method daily. One day, after I had been practicing for seven days, I left home at 6:30 a.m. to start my day full day: accompany my youngest son to the DMV to take his driving test, drive him to school, get a car smog check, go downtown to LA to get clinic supplies, pick up my son from school at 2:30 p.m., eat lunch at home, drop my son off at his track competition, go back home to cook dinner, go out again to pick up my son ...it was a hectic day.

Usually, during my menopause period, my body couldn't stand that full schedule, but a miracle happened on that day. I didn't feel drained at all. Actually, I felt alive with inner strength, just like when I was twenty-five, the first time coming to live in LA. I felt young and fearless, full of energy. It was an incredible experience that made me clear my aka cord and weed out the junk data and reset. Disconnecting allows us to reconnect and reset and reach more profound wisdom that will refill us and return us to our lives, renewing our sense of novelty, enthusiasm, and freshness.

One night near the end of Spring, an eighty-six year old Native American spiritual leader invited me to join their Pow Wow dance ceremony, offering Mother Earth prayers. Native American military veterans led the grand entry, and elders and tribes in colorful regalia followed. Then the Circle Dance invited spectators to join in. The final dance was the sacred Bear Dance. I can still feel the energy that coursed through my whole body while they danced slowly and quietly from dark spaces into the circle. I felt overwhelmingly moved.

Before the ceremony started, the spiritual leader brought me into the circle's center, a beautiful warm campfire. He taught me how to give the offering according to their ritual, and he asked me,

"What do you see while you are standing here? Look around you, what do you see and feel?"

I looked throughout and saw the outer circle crowded with people, but the inside was empty, quiet, and time slowed down; only the campfire at the center was burning. I told him my observation.

He asked, "Any other observations? Use your heart to feel, not your brain to think..."

I calmed myself down and looked around again; suddenly, I felt so peaceful, standing in the center. And I felt myself floating in the universe; outside, the noisy crowds of people looked like many stars and planets orbiting around me, and I was the center of the universe!

The center campfire looked like the sun, and I was at the center of this universe! Immediately I understood! In silence, I connected with the Divine, and I feel complete, peaceful, and satisfied. The famous Chinese phrase: "The heart must be quiet to live with wisdom. The body must keep active to promote the positive energy of living." I understood that everything comes from our hearts and thoughts and that I am the only one who is fully responsible for me, and that this is a sign of strength. I have to heal myself, take care of myself, and love myself, and then I can help others.

But I also know that no matter how deep a person's understanding of the truth of the Universe is, on this Earth, life continues, and there will be many challenges. Just like a pilot flying through turbulence, I need to keep my plane in control while not losing sight of my destination. That's why I have to be patient with myself and willing to practice the "Clearing method" again and again. Going through these different levels also helps me face crises and obstacles with more insight. Living this way helps me grow inexperience, and I can know myself more deeply, which allows me to release unhealthy attachments.

I am precious and priceless. Now, whenever I feel overwhelmed by heavy emotions or thoughts, I recall that memorable night in the campfire circle, connecting with the center of silence within, connecting to my inner self. When I feel and identify my negative emotions, I start "clearing" by repeating those four magic sentences repeatedly. Then, all I have to do is be patient and quiet and listen to the Divine messages that help me follow my inner compass and lead me to a better life.

Through years of research, practice, and my personal experience of acupuncture and energy medicine, I have repeatedly broken through the mind's boundaries using self-healing methods. Every breakthrough has made me more humble, and I have surrendered to the Universe's power, which always moves and is grateful.

I look back and know it was all worth it.

My favorite tips for clearing the database and resetting the mind

- Identify the emotion you are experiencing and wish to clear.
- Take full responsibility and face the emotion.
- Repeat the four sentences below, add your name at the beginning of those four sentences to be more exact.

  (Insert name)
  I am sorry
  Forgive me
  Thank you
  I love you

- Send blessings for myself and for someone who makes me feel the emotion.

Tips of Iceburgs

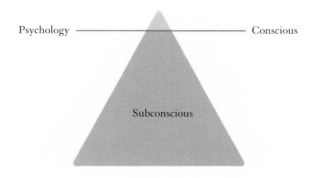

Psychology ———————— Conscious

Subconscious

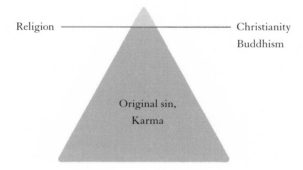

Religion ———————— Christianity
Buddhism

Original sin,
Karma

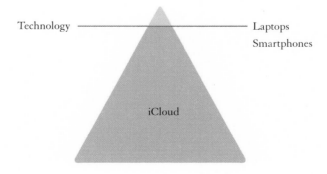

Technology ———————— Laptops
Smartphones

iCloud

The Next Step

Cure sometimes, treat often,
comfort always.

Hippocrates

I had a patient who was fighting third-stage breast cancer for eight years. She was five years older than me and thin, elegant, and calm. She came to the clinic once a week regularly for her last two years of life. She felt that acupuncture helped her to manage body pain. After chemo, she would experience loss of appetite, abdominal bloating, nausea, and pain; after acupuncture, she could start energizing and eating well again.

I remembered that it was in January; we had just gotten back from our New Year's vacation. We sat down in my clinic as usual, and she told me calmly but with tears in her eyes, "Doctor Lee, my latest cancer examination report came out; the result was bad. Cancer cells have metastasized to my lungs, lymphatic system, and liver. The oncologist told me that I only have one month left."

The air froze between us. I held on her hands, speechless, tears welling up in my eyes. A minute passed, and I took a big breath and spoke in a relaxed tone,

"Okay, let's see if acupuncture can do more for you. At least it can help to manage your pain and bring some quality to life at the end. I will do my best."

She moved into hospice care at home. She kept coming to my clinic for acupuncture twice a week. Gradually I booked more time for her during treatments so we could spend more quality time together. Every time she came, I checked her pulse and tongue thoroughly, asked detailed questions, and tracked down any clues that might cause an imbalance in her body. I tried extending that balance for as long as possible, thus extending her life.

One day, I asked her, "Do you ever talk to your body?"

"Talk to my body? No." She replied with a puzzled expression on her face.

I couldn't help but blame myself. How come I hadn't introduced the inner strength and spiritual healing? In TCM, we address the importance of the concept, "Unity of Man and Heaven," meaning "Harmony of Man and Nature," we should know we are the oneness, we are already in heaven, we are at home, and a clear spirit and mind help manage our physical body.

I started to add more time to each treatment session so we'd have enough time to talk and so that I could help guide her in exploring her inner world and help her build up a dialogue with her body and spirit. Because if we are to overcome severe illnesses such as cancer, we must develop the ability to self-check to change our inner and outer world completely. Try to be a new person and give yourself a second chance of living.

TCM described that our kidneys are the natural source, and the spleen is the acquired foundation. From my understanding, it's like our savings account and checking account; our parents' genes are in our savings, so we'd better keep it. Our spleen and stomach are our checking account, with content going in and out frequently. We eat meals every day, transform food into energy, and use it for daily activities. (I have often observed that when patients recover slightly, they are so happy that they over-use their bodies immediately. They use up all their energy and become ill again. It is similar to when we get our paycheck and then happily spend it all.)

Patients with cancer especially need to take good care of their spleen and stomach systems, and if the body can digest, absorb, and defecate, it can survive. The essential diet for ill people is rice congee. This rice congee must be boiled for about two hours until it turns gelatine, helping gastrointestinal function. This rice congee has become an essential diet for the sick person for more than two thousand years in Asia.

She was too weak to cook at the time, and I cooked congee for her. Every time she came for treatment, she would take a pot of congee home. That was the only period I cooked congee so diligently in my life.

Five months passed, which exceeded the original one-month life expectancy of the oncologist. Our friendship grew, but she became thinner and weaker. When she came to the clinic, she was fragile and it was difficult for her to lie down on the treatment table. We adjusted for a while, trying to find a comfortable position for her. She had pulmonary edema due to cancer cells' metastasis, and she would often have severe coughs once lying down. She coughed and coughed, so I grew worried. I carefully discussed the treatment plan with her and asked,

"Do you think acupuncture is still helping you?"

"Yes, I don't need to take the morphine and other medicines that my oncologist doctors prepared for me anymore," she said. "Every time after the needles, I can sleep better, and my mind feels clear and calm. It makes me very comfortable. But I've noticed that the effectiveness is reducing from five days to about two to three days."

For her convenience, the hospice care bed in her home was adjustable; the soft bed made her comfortable and put her at ease, so I went to her home for treatments. A month later, I increased visits from two days a week to three days a week. At this time, her edema gradually crept from her feet to her knees and abdomen region. Therefore, I only inserted needles on her hands and scalp, where the skin wasn't swollen. Unexpectedly, the scalp needles had an incredible effect. Two weeks before her death, she had a caregiver stay by her side all day. On several occasions, as soon as I entered the house, the caregiver would rush to me and report that she was very anxious and irritable and didn't know how to make her feel better. But each time after the scalp needles were inserted, the patient would close her eyes and fall asleep within three minutes.

During the last six months of accompanying her, I stopped listening to pop music on the radio. I started listening to religious music, worshipping Divine power, and sending prayers; it comforted me. I cried whenever I thought of her; although I am fully aware that this is the natural way of life, it still took a toll on me emotionally. I sought psychological counseling twice during that time, and I blamed myself for not saving her life. I may treat some illnesses and diseases, but I cannot stop death in the end. Lives are in the hands of the higher power. And this is proof that no one can control when God decides to take a life away.

At the time, every Monday during the month before this breast cancer patient's death, I received text messages from multiple patients' families informing me of a patient's passing. For five weeks in a row, I lost a patient every Monday. It broke my heart. Four of them were cancer patients, and one died from pneumonia. Now, she also came to the end of life. I noticed that the acupuncture effects were not lasting as long as they had before; I had even reached the limitation of the number of times I could visit and treat her at home. I had a feeling that she was leaving soon in a day.

On my way to our last visit, I went to a flower shop to pick a beautiful orchid for her. I put it next to her Bible and said, "I am here to say goodbye. After I leave today, I might not see you again. If you are uncomfortable tomorrow, please take morphine! Do not resist it. Just try and make yourself comfortable, stay in peace, and embark on a new journey. Angels will be here to guide you to heaven; you are not alone. You are such a brave life warrior. Thank you for letting me accompany you on this journey, for letting me witness the great effect of acupuncture and scalp needles. Thank you!"

She smiled with tears and said, "Hurry...The bills...Do I still owe you any medical expenses? Let me pay you now."

Both of us just laughed out loud. We gave each other one last hug and said goodbye.

At four o'clock the next morning, I received a text from her caregiver, informing me that she had passed peacefully.

In the process of accompanying the deaths of several cancer patients, it seems that instead of helping treat them, I'm allowing myself to heal.

One morning, as usual, the way to leave the community was quite busy. Everyone was driving fast and rushing to their jobs. Instead of following them, I drove my son in the opposite direction and headed back home from his early morning track training at the school. We were happily chatting when I saw a little squirrel about ten meters ahead. The little squirrel was planning to cross the road to enter the field on the other side. I immediately stepped on the brakes and shouted, "Little squirrel, don't rush! I'll let you pass, but the other lane is full of speeding vehicles...!"

While shouting, I saw the little squirrel run forward. It rushed past the front of my car, and it didn't slow down, didn't stop and watch, just ran full speed ahead. When it jumped over and passed my car, I saw from the rear view mirror that it happened to be smashed by a car in that opposite lane. In an instant, it was gone. My God! Tears fell down my face, and I cried, "No...No...No... What is this world? The little squirrel just wanted to go back to the field, but it is flattened in an instant, no more! Why did this happen in front of me? Why? Why?"

I kept crying and crying. My son understood my feelings and was quiet, did not say a word, letting me cry all the way back home.

After returning home and dropping off my son, I turned to go to work again. I still couldn't hold my tears and think, "I don't want to go that way. Maybe I should take a different route. I can't stand to see the death scene of the little squirrel. It's too sad. I can't take it. Maybe I should find another way to the clinic."

While driving out of the community, I was still struggling to evaluate,

"Hmm! A detour might add ten minutes to my drive, and my patients may be waiting outside the clinic, so it's not a good idea to take another route."

Then it occurred to me that this was a pattern of behavior in my life. Whenever I had a sorrowful problem that I couldn't solve, I chose to go the other way. Was this running away? Runaway, again and again, did I want to keep running away? Or could I bravely face my fears and resolve them? Okay! I told myself: "Be pragmatic, calm down, work is important, don't let this mess up your whole day. Just take the routine road!"

When I drove by the little squirrel's death location, I was ready to close my eyes and rush by. I didn't want to see the carnage. Unexpectedly, though, when I drove past, there was no trace of the little squirrel. It was like nothing had happened. I looked more challenging, trying to find the remains of the little squirrel. Oh my! All the vehicles rushing to work and took away pieces of the squirrel as they drove past. I felt hopeless and quickly continued going to work. I knew I couldn't do anything but pray for the little squirrel.

What was the sign sent from above? To not obsess over things, to not grow overly attached to something that passes like clouds? A quote from the Heart Mandra passed through my mind: "This world is like a dream bubble."

But, the literature's wisdom could not assuage my emotions; however, for the next week, I felt sad when thinking about this little squirrel. I cried when I talked to my friend about this squirrel and felt sorrow whenever I drove by the accident location.

My friend said,"If that were a cat that had been killed by a car, I would be as sad as you, but I can't be sorry about the squirrel."

"Why?" I asked.

"Because squirrels always come to my yard to eat the fruit from my tree. They take bites from all the fruits and make me mad!"

What strikes one person's sympathy can cause another person's anger. My friend and I talked about the same subject but with different emotional reactions. Buddha taught that in this world, everything is "neutral," and that's why we should not make judgments because each person's point of view is different. There is always some reason for our mindset. Everything is cause and effect.

The death of the little squirrel recalled my childhood memory of seeing my little puppy hit by a car and killed. My little puppy had slipped out of the house and into the street, and I couldn't save him. I also remembered the other stray puppies that I hadn't been able to save or take care of. Every one of those memories caused such pain; why did this keep happening again and again? Were there some messages for me to explore?

I went to my psychic counselor, and she helped me with a session of guided meditation. She helped me see many animals and people who had been saved, taken care of, and healed by me. They had a good time with me when they were alive, even though they eventually died. My psychic counselor helped me process the guilt I had left in my heart - just because I could not save them from death. They came over and told me one by one: "Don't feel guilty, don't blame yourself. Life and death are like air in the sky: they are natural, completing the circle of life. Please don't worry. You have done your part. We all came to tell you, thank you! Please don't keep feeling guilty, for this guilt is like an invisible cord still keeping us together. Please, let go so that we can go to the place where we need to be."

When I drove back home from the consultant's office that night and passed by the little squirrel's death location, suddenly, my heart was no longer sad and tangled. Instead, it was full of deep love, and I prayed,

"Thank you! Thank you, little squirrel. Rest in peace. I am in peace too."

Oneness & Wholeness

Yin and Yang, good and bad, visible and invisible, physical and emotional, matter and spirit...They will always be together.

People have the free will to choose which side we want to be on. Or, if we are wise and strong, we do not need to choose, but only surrender to oneness.

Self-awareness comes from within. Wholeness makes our reality, the crisis is a blessing in disguise.

Dr. Jessie Lee

In his last year of junior high school, my youngest boy bravely chose by himself to go live in Germany with my sister and study abroad due to a complication in his U.S. resident documents. He was fourteen years old and had never left me before. The coming separation heavily stressed both of us for almost six months.

The day I drove him to the German Embassy in downtown Los Angeles for his German student visa interview. The interview appointment was at 10:00 a.m. We left home at 6:00 a.m. to avoid the infamous traffic of LA. My son slept the entire time while I was driving and listening to music. After two tedious hours, we neared downtown, and the GPS guided me off the freeway to take local routes. When my car was crossing the bridge into LA, I suddenly saw myself floating above the vehicle. I watched myself drive in slow motion, and the panorama of the city was pale yellow and quiet.

"What the heck!" I exclaimed. "What's this? Am I dreaming?"

I looked around. In sight was the beautiful city skyline, a dog, and a homeless person sleeping by the roadside. I said to myself, "That homeless man is me, that dog is me, all of LA is me. Wow! Everything is me!! The sky, the cars, the bridge, everything is me."

Tears fell down my face. I couldn't tell how long I was in the slow-motion space, maybe just one second. But I met a great wholeness; I met the eternal.

I Am The I, "I" come forth from the void into a light; I am the breath that nurtures life, I am that emptiness, that hollowness beyond all consciousness, The I, the Id, the All. I draw my bow of rainbows across the waters, The continuum of minds with matters. I am the incoming and outgoing of breath, The invisible, untouchable breeze, The undefinable atom of creation. I am the I. (- From *SITH Ho'oponopono*).

Ever since this incredible and unique experience, my inner interactions with others have changed. When I am with patients in the clinic, my internal boundaries are open, and I fully connect to them and their pain, both good and bad. The bad part is that I have all kinds of issues after clinic work. The good thing is that I have fully committed to myself the self-healing pathway; I understand that I have to heal myself before I help others, which taught me a very disciplined lifestyle, including going to bed before 11:00 p.m., eating healthy meals, managing stress, and allowing relaxation time for myself.

Years of experience in the clinic have made me understand that if the patients do not practice introspection but only have their physicians unblock their energy, their energy becomes congested. Because the real treatment is not a request from the outside, to balance the body and mind, you can only rely on your own "inner seeking of the law" to repair. Self-awareness comes from within.

Physicians can only assist you, but we can't do homework for you. It is like a saying: "The master leads you into the door, and you do the practice individually". We can't be full by only watching others. The real healing is to go back inside and keep clearing all impurities until we are like innocent children once more. The end of the road is our supreme self-sufficiency, our healing source.

My self-healing journey has led me to explore every different angle of this planet. I keep opening my mind to learning, and Divinity has never disappointed me. It has always brought a teacher to guide me.

While studying the written theories in my NGH Hypnosis Certification training courses, they validated many of the beautiful sensory experiences I have had repeatedly. These sorts of "mysterious" experiences are also found in the ancient Chinese medical field called Zhu-You[1], or the "Blessing Talking Singing Healing" technique. It was called witchcraft in ancient times. However, back then, it was seen as a noble profession and was an official name given by the Xuanyuan Yellow Emperor (BC.2717-2599). Those who were able to perform the healing at that time were highly respected. Most of the methods are taught by the master to the student directly. "I am told that in ancient times when a physician treated a disease, he only transferred the patient's thought and spirit to sever the source of the disease. Nowadays, the patient is treated with herbs internally and acupuncture externally. Nevertheless, some of the diseases are cured. Still, some of them cannot be cued" (Chapter 13, "On the Therapy of Transferring Thought and Spirit," The Yellow Emperor's Canon of Internal Medicine).

1. Zhu-You 祝由 is a healing method that integrates the patient's body and spirit to suppress the disease's occurrence and development by analyzing the patient's biological field until the illness subsides. The ancients developed this healing method to communicate with the Universe. Mastering this mysterious form of communication can directionally mobilize the Universe into serving the human body and mind. On the surface, this practice can seem completely superstitious. Still, it is the most primitive psychotherapy that we now know through quantum physics based on certain scientific principles. If the energy resonance effect is good, patients can achieve the therapeutic effect. Any language spoken in a calm and relaxed manner can treat various diseases, but the language must be positive, and there should be no malicious or pathological thoughts. The universal truth always tells us the same thing using different modalities and different terminologies according to different regions on the Earth and different cultures.

During my NGH Hypnosis Certification training courses, I have met my four-year-old self and comforted her fear of being alone at night time. How amazing that once I integrated and healed that part of myself so I am no longer afraid to be alone at night-time at age fifty! Is it the "parallel universe" effect? A "pass-through" effect synchronized? Does time travel?

Even in science, different scientists have different definitions and explanations for the concept of a parallel universe, but I believe in the "parallel Universe" effect from my personal experiences. The word multiverse is often used in cosmology to convey multiple parallel universes. In other words, the world we exist in is just one in time and space, and there are parallel existences in the multiverse. We all live in a subsection of the poetry of this multiverse.

Another day in the Hypnosis Certification training course, we practiced guided meditation to meet our inner child again. The teacher asked us to guess which inner child we were going to meet this time. I thought maybe I would meet myself at age thirty-five because that was a traumatic year for my marriage. But I met my thirteen-year-old self. Why? During a significant change in my life journey, I went to live in Bolivia. This version of me came with long hair and was entirely innocent and fearless, an extroverted girl jumping to sit in front of fifty-year-old me. My tears streamed down my face, the most profound emotions coming as soon as I saw my thirteen-year-old self.

My teacher kept guiding me.

"What do you want to say now that you see her? Tell her something, give some message to the young you."

"Hmm...I don't know. I don't know what to say..." Everything was just happening so fast, and I hadn't prepared anything to say.

Then, a sudden message came to me, and I told her,

"Be patient! Be prepared! Always have faith!"

My young self suddenly looked like she got the message and became serious, paying attention to my words.

Our teacher explained to me after guiding me back to the present, "Now, you saw your thirteen-year-old self listen to your message. In that space, since she took this advice in mind and as long as she keeps living, do you think when she is thirty-five, she will meet the same trauma as you had in this life?"

Of course not! She listened, so she would be more mature and patient and wary about getting married too young too fast. She would have more time to get to know her husband better, would know how to communicate with him. Then, the drama at thirty-five wouldn't happen. Her life would be smoother and happier, and her good vibes could resonate back to the future and affect me. That's amazing!

That day we were assigned homework, we were to use the self-guided meditation technique to meet again with our younger self. But this time, we were to listen and focus on what they wanted to say to us.

I always liked doing homework right away as soon as I got home. So I started the self-guidance. Then the thirteen-year-old me came again, but this time came with a guitar. The thirteen-year-old me looked elegant and thoughtful. She sat down calmly, arranged her guitar, and began to sing a song for me.

I concentrated hard to try and listen to the melody. I could hardly understand anything except for a few words: "youth, energetic, song."

And she gave me her message, "Be brave, stay youthful, have love and energy, go with Faith."

After returning from the meditation state, I immediately checked Google and Yotube to try to find any clue of this song. Bingo! I found it within a minute. The music existed! Incredible! When I played the song, I could immediately sing along. I knew this song thirty-seven years ago. That song was not my favorite song, but I sang it a few times when I was thirteen. After she gave me that message, I could play the guitar and sing that song again. I had inner strength increasing, calm and peace restored. What a stunning lesson! I closed my eyes and kept thinking.

Everything Can Be
A Healing Remedy

I have explored and experimented
with herbal supplements, vitamins,
medications; flower essences, sound
therapy, aura soma, crystal healing,
power animals, and more.

All kinds of spirit medicines help with
healing, and now with a renewed
commitment to wash and clear inner
negativities, finally, I have become
healthier and lighter.

Dr. Jessie Lee

I was nearing the end of this book, but I suddenly paused for almost three months. I thought about how to end it all, and there was no way to continue. At the time, I could only surrender, hold my temper, be open to the message from heaven above, and see where the universe's power would take me. What is my task to accomplish and to share?

So, once again, through every kind of problem that suddenly appeared in life, I let this experience strengthen my self-discipline. Each time I broke through my boundary, I see a clear, unique life pattern.

To know our natural-born physiques as our destiny, we can help ourselves by continually learning, correcting, revising, and doing more. There are many systems believed to determine our life paths in East and West countries in ancient and modern times. The methods include Chinese I-Ching Bagua, 5Y6Q, Purple Star Astrology fortune-telling, the twelve zodiacs, twelve constellations, numerology, tarot cards, crystal reading with healing oracles, and more. All these can often accurately provide a foreseeing of our life destiny laws; each system has its jaw-dropping precision. However, if our fate is doomed, then what's the exciting part of life? Do we follow destiny and tide to complete this life?

However, for many Eastern and Western great thinkers, educators, and religious scholars, it seems to be not "fatalism" for thousands of years. Through my life experience, I met the essence of the Buddha's teaching that "The mind creates the matter," and Christ's "I am the way and the truth and the life," and New Age Spiritualism, "You create your reality."

On earth, it's about the concept of Yin and Yang, good and bad, gods and devils, and this is the kind of dynamic that needed to be balanced, and there will always be a Yin and Yang rotation; we choose this or that in every moment, every thought. It's our choice, and we can choose to ascend to a higher energy body, and then, we break through this relative constraint.

I want to share the story of ancient truth with the practical method that helped me a lot. It's the book "Liao Fan's Si Xun" (Liao Fan's Four Principles). When I was twenty-five years old, I thought it was just common sense and old sayings. I didn't take it seriously and didn't take action. Until I began doing my doctoral energy medicine research, the Universe revealed truths to me through countless great predecessors and scientists. When I learned the operation of various energies, I knew that the idea was about the energy waves again and logically explained and proven. Influenced by the healing power and the self-purification I practice in daily life, the power of change happened quickly.

In the Ming Dynasty of China, a minister called Yuan Liao Fan (1533 - 1606) wrote the classic Liao Fan's Four Principles as an heirloom. It has become a very famous saint's book in the Chinese community. When Mr. Yuan was young, he asked a master to calculate his fate before attending a government examination. Though it was theoretically precise, Mr. Yuan believed he could not change his life pattern and that he would die at the young age of fifty-three, with no children.

Then, in 1569, Mr. Yuan met a Zen master named Yungu, who taught and explained fate to Yuan:

"If we actively help others and think the right way, we can change our destiny."

And minister Yuan not only lived past fifty-three years old but also had two sons.

At the age of sixty-nine, he wrote Liao Fan's Four Principles.

The first principle of training is to learn that the "destiny of man can be created by oneself, not by fate."

The second principal training is to repent and avoid small mistakes; thus, it will naturally prevent bigger mistakes.

The third principal training is to be on the side of goodness - when doing good deeds to help others, good things will accumulate, and fate will naturally change. Because we are part of the Oneness, when I am right and helping others, I am also helping myself build a better world where everyone benefits.

The fourth principal training is the effect of humility - getting along with others, being modest, and learning from others, will naturally lead to progress.

Each day he wrote down his merits and demerits, recorded his thoughts and behaviors, made a general review of himself, and reminded himself to correct his mistakes. According to Mr. Yuan, this daily practice plants good seeds and can harvest good fruits after a while. It is a very effective way to change our lives and also make the world better. Mr. Yuan successfully modified his destiny; he lived to be seventy-four years old (he passed in AC 1608) with two sons.

I learned from him; I have a little notebook with two columns to record my positive and negative thoughts with a simple line; calculated and compared at the end of each day to see how many positive and negative thoughts I have. Watching the thoughts helped to build out my awareness.

Another modern business book that helped a lot in my life-changing is The Diamond Cutter by Michael Roach. For the past twenty-five years, it has helped me see where I needed to change and take action in my daily life. The "six-hour checklist note" taught in the book is also an efficient practice guide. Clear thought can generate more specific energies in writing down goals, and the power that pushes us upward can become stable and moved manageably.

But the first step of "self-purification" is the most important. The thoughts that are invisible to the naked eye are very energetic. Don't underestimate "thoughts." The energy of every thought and behavior has been recorded, saved in the sea of consciousness's energy cloud.

Taking action, always practicing, repeating, correcting myself, being grateful, and giving blessings and feedback to this world has helped me evolve from a sorrowful homemaker full of illnesses to an Oriental Medicine doctor and acupuncturist healthy inside and out.

Everything can be a healing remedy starting from one little thought.

I have a sign hanging on my clinic wall, 2/168. The "2" represents the amount of time – two hours – that I spend, on average, with each patient during a visit. The "168" represents the number of hours in a week. This sign is there to remind patients that they are responsible for taking care of themselves for the majority of the week's hours, and they can do this by using the power of self-healing.

If Only I Had Changed Myself First

(Written on the tomb of an Anglican Bishop in the crypts of Westminster Abbey in London, England. Compliments of Chris Boyd.)

When I was young and free, and my imagination had no limits, I dreamed of changing the world. As I grew older and wiser, I realized the world would not change, and I decided to shorten my sights somewhat and change only my country. But, it too seemed immovable. As I entered my twilight years, in one last desperate attempt, I sought to change only my family, those closest to me, but alas, they would have none of it.

Now I lie here on my deathbed and realize, perhaps for the first time, that if only I had changed myself first, then by example, I may have influenced my family, and with their encouragement and support, I may have bettered my country, and who knows, I may have changed the world.

Printed in Taiwan, Republic of China

For information address:

Elephant White Cultural Enterprise Ltd. Press,

8F.-2, No.1, Keji Rd., Dali Dist., Taichung City 41264, Taiwan (R.O.C.)

Distributed by Elephant White Cultural Enterprise Co., Ltd.

ISBN: 978-626-7056-54-7

Suggested Price: **NT$750**